ALDOUS HUXLEY

*

Mortal Coils

By ALDOUS HUXLEY

Novels

CROME YELLOW *
ANTIC HAY *
THOSE BARREN LEAVES *
POINT COUNTER POINT *
BRAVE NEW WORLD
EYELESS IN GAZA *
AFTER MANY A SUMMER
TIME MUST HAVE A STOP
APE AND ESSENCE

Short Stories

LIMBO *
MORTAL COILS *
LITTLE MEXICAN *
TWO OR THREE GRACES *
BRIEF CANDLES *

Biography

GREY EMINENCE

Essays and Belles Lettres

ON THE MARGIN *
ALONG THE ROAD *
PROPER STUDIES *
DO WHAT YOU WILL *
MUSIC AT NIGHT & *
VULGARITY IN LITERATURE
TEXTS AND PRETEXTS (Anthology) *
THE OLIVE TREE *
ENDS AND MEANS (An Enquiry into the Nature of Ideals) *
THE ART OF SEEING
THE PERENNIAL PHILOSOPHY
SCIENCE, LIBERTY AND PEACE

Travel

JESTING PILATE (Illustrated) *
BEYOND THE MEXIQUE BAY (Illustrated) *

Poetry and Drama

VERSES AND A COMEDY *
(including early poems, Leda, The Cicadas and The World of Light, a Comedy)
THE GIOCONDA SMILE

* *Issued in this Collected Edition*

ALDOUS HUXLEY

Mortal Coils

Five Stories

1949
Chatto & Windus
LONDON

PUBLISHED BY
Chatto & Windus
LONDON
*
Clarke, Irwin & Company Ltd
TORONTO

Applications regarding translation rights in any work by Aldous Huxley should be addressed to Chatto & Windus, 40 William IV Street, London, W.C. 2

FIRST PUBLISHED 1922
FIRST ISSUED IN THIS COLLECTED
EDITION 1949
PRINTED IN GREAT BRITAIN

CONTENTS

Some of these stories have appeared in the following papers: *The Cornhill*, *The English Review*, *Coterie*. My thanks are due to the Editors of these journals for permission to reprint.

THE GIOCONDA SMILE

I

"MISS SPENCE will be down directly, sir."

"Thank you," said Mr. Hutton, without turning round. Janet Spence's parlourmaid was so ugly—ugly on purpose, it always seemed to him, malignantly, criminally ugly—that he could not bear to look at her more than was necessary. The door closed. Left to himself, Mr. Hutton got up and began to wander round the room, looking with meditative eyes at the familiar objects it contained.

Photographs of Greek statuary, photographs of the Roman Forum, coloured prints of Italian masterpieces, all very safe and well known. Poor, dear Janet, what a prig—what an intellectual snob! Her real taste was illustrated in that water-colour by the pavement artist, the one she had paid half a crown for (and thirty-five shillings for the frame). How often he had heard her tell the story, how often expatiate on the beauties of that skilful imitation of an oleograph! "A real Artist in the streets," and you could hear the capital A in Artist as she spoke the words. She made you feel that part of his glory had entered into Janet Spence when she tendered him that half-crown for the copy of the oleograph. She was implying a compliment to her own taste and penetration. A genuine Old Master for half a crown. Poor, dear Janet!

Mr. Hutton came to a pause in front of a small oblong mirror. Stooping a little to get a full view of his face, he passed a white, well-manicured finger over his moustache. It was as curly, as freshly auburn as it had been twenty years ago. His hair still retained its colour, and there was no sign of baldness yet—only a certain elevation of the brow. "Shakespearean," thought Mr. Hutton, with a smile, as he surveyed the smooth and polished expanse of his forehead.

Others abide our question, thou art free. . . . Footsteps in the sea . . . Majesty. . . . Shakespeare, thou shouldst be living at this hour. No, that was Milton, wasn't it? Milton, the Lady of Christ's. There was no lady about him. He was what the women would call a manly man. That was why they liked him—for the curly auburn moustache and the discreet redolence of tobacco. Mr. Hutton smiled again; he enjoyed making fun of himself. Lady of Christ's? No, no. He was the Christ of Ladies. Very pretty, very pretty. The Christ of Ladies. Mr. Hutton wished there were somebody he could tell the joke to. Poor, dear Janet wouldn't appreciate it, alas!

He straightened himself up, patted his hair, and resumed his peregrination. Damn the Roman Forum; he hated those dreary photographs.

Suddenly he became aware that Janet Spence was in the room, standing near the door. Mr. Hutton started, as though he had been taken in some felonious act. To make these silent and spectral appearances was one of Janet Spence's peculiar talents. Perhaps she had been there all the time, had seen him looking at himself in the mirror. Impossible! But, still, it was disquieting.

"Oh, you gave me such a surprise," said Mr. Hutton, recovering his smile and advancing with outstretched hand to meet her.

Miss Spence was smiling too: her

Gioconda smile, he had once called it in a moment of half-ironical flattery. Miss Spence had taken the compliment seriously, and always tried to live up to the Leonardo standard. She smiled on in silence while Mr. Hutton shook hands; that was part of the Gioconda business.

"I hope you're well," said Mr. Hutton. "You look it."

What a queer face she had! That small mouth pursed forward by the Gioconda expression into a little snout with a round hole in the middle as though for whistling—it was like a penholder seen from the front. Above the mouth a well-shaped nose, finely aquiline. Eyes large, lustrous, and dark, with the largeness, lustre, and darkness that seems to invite sties and an occasional bloodshot suffusion. They were fine eyes, but unchangingly grave. The penholder might do its Gioconda trick, but the eyes never altered in their earnestness. Above them, a pair of boldly arched, heavily pencilled black eyebrows lent a surprising air of power, as of a Roman matron, to the upper portion of the face. Her hair was dark and equally Roman; Agrippina from the brows upward.

"I thought I'd just look in on my way home," Mr. Hutton went on. "Ah, it's good to be back here"—he indicated with a wave of his hand the flowers in the vases, the sunshine and greenery beyond the windows—"it's good to be back in the country after a stuffy day of business in town."

Miss Spence, who had sat down, pointed to a chair at her side.

"No, really, I can't sit down," Mr. Hutton protested. "I must get back to see how poor Emily is. She was rather seedy this morning." He sat down, nevertheless. "It's these wretched liver chills. She's always getting them. Women——" He broke off and coughed, so as to hide the fact that he had uttered. He was about to say that women with weak digestions ought not to marry; but the remark was too cruel, and he didn't really believe it. Janet Spence, moreover, was a believer in eternal flames and spiritual attachments. "She hopes to be well enough," he added, "to see you at luncheon to-morrow. Can you come? Do!" He smiled persuasively. "It's my invitation too, you know."

She dropped her eyes, and Mr. Hutton almost thought that he detected a certain reddening of the cheek. It was a tribute ; he stroked his moustache.

"I should like to come if you think Emily's really well enough to have a visitor."

"Of course. You'll do her good. You'll do us both good. In married life three is often better company than two."

"Oh, you're cynical."

Mr. Hutton always had a desire to say "Bow-wow-wow" whenever that last word was spoken. It irritated him more than any other word in the language. But instead of barking he made haste to protest.

"No, no. I'm only speaking a melancholy truth. Reality doesn't always come up to the ideal, you know. But that doesn't make me believe any the less in the ideal. Indeed, I believe in it passionately—the ideal of a matrimony between two people in perfect accord. I think it's realisable. I'm sure it is."

He paused significantly and looked at her with an arch expression. A virgin of thirty-six, but still unwithered ; she had her charms. And there was something really rather enigmatic about her. Miss Spence made no reply, but continued to smile. There were times when Mr.

Hutton got rather bored with the Gioconda. He stood up.

"I must really be going now. Farewell, mysterious Gioconda." The smile grew intenser, focused itself, as it were, in a narrower snout. Mr. Hutton made a Cinquecento gesture, and kissed her extended hand. It was the first time he had done such a thing; the action seemed not to be resented. "I look forward to to-morrow."

"Do you?"

For answer Mr. Hutton once more kissed her hand, then turned to go. Miss Spence accompanied him to the porch.

"Where's your car?" she asked.

"I left it at the gate of the drive."

"I'll come and see you off."

"No, no." Mr. Hutton was playful, but determined. "You must do no such thing. I simply forbid you."

"But I should like to come," Miss Spence protested, throwing a rapid Gioconda at him.

Mr. Hutton held up his hand. "No," he repeated, and then, with a gesture that was almost the blowing of a kiss, he started to run down the drive, lightly, on his toes, with long, bounding strides like a boy's. He was proud of that run; it was quite marvellously youthful. Still, he was glad the drive was no longer. At the last bend, before passing out of sight of the house, he halted and turned round. Miss Spence was still standing on the steps, smiling her smile. He waved his hand, and this time quite definitely and overtly wafted a kiss in her direction. Then, breaking once more into his magnificent canter, he rounded the last dark promontory of trees. Once out of sight of the house he let his high paces decline to a trot, and finally to a walk. He took out his handkerchief and began wiping his neck inside his collar. What fools, what fools! Had there ever been such an ass as poor, dear Janet Spence? Never, unless it was himself. Decidedly he was the more malignant fool, since he, at least, was aware of his folly and still persisted in it. Why did he persist? Ah, the problem that was himself, the problem that was other people . . .

He had reached the gate. A large, prosperous-looking motor was standing at the side of the road.

"Home, M'Nab." The chauffeur touched his cap. "And stop at the cross-roads on the way, as usual," Mr. Hutton added, as he opened the door of the car. "Well?" he said, speaking into the obscurity that lurked within.

"Oh, Teddy Bear, what an age you've been!" It was a fresh and childish voice that spoke the words. There was the faintest hint of Cockney impurity about the vowel sounds.

Mr. Hutton bent his large form and darted into the car with the agility of an animal regaining its burrow.

"Have I?" he said, as he shut the door. The machine began to move. "You must have missed me a lot if you found the time so long." He sat back in the low seat; a cherishing warmth enveloped him.

"Teddy Bear . . ." and with a sigh of contentment a charming little head declined on to Mr. Hutton's shoulder. Ravished, he looked down sideways at the round, babyish face.

"Do you know, Doris, you look like the pictures of Louise de Kerouaille." He passed his fingers through a mass of curly hair.

"Who's Louise de Kera-whatever-it-is?" Doris spoke from remote distances.

"She was, alas! *Fuit.* We shall all be 'was' one of these days. Meanwhile . . ."

Mr. Hutton covered the babyish face with kisses. The car rushed smoothly along. M'Nab's back, through the front window, was stonily impassive, the back of a statue.

"Your hands," Doris whispered. "Oh, you mustn't touch me. They give me electric shocks."

Mr. Hutton adored her for the virgin imbecility of the words. How late in one's existence one makes the discovery of one's body!

"The electricity isn't in me, it's in you." He kissed her again, whispering her name several times: Doris, Doris, Doris. The scientific appellation of the sea-mouse, he was thinking as he kissed the throat she offered him, white and extended like the throat of a victim awaiting the sacrificial knife. The sea-mouse was a sausage with iridescent fur: very peculiar. Or was Doris the sea-cucumber, which turns itself inside out in moments of alarm? He would really have to go to Naples again, just to see the aquarium. These sea creatures were fabulous, unbelievably fantastic.

"Oh, Teddy Bear!" (More zoology;

but he was only a land animal. His poor little jokes!) "Teddy Bear, I'm so happy."

"So am I," said Mr. Hutton. Was it true?

"But I wish I knew if it were right. Tell me, Teddy Bear, is it right or wrong?"

"Ah, my dear, that's just what I've been wondering for the last thirty years."

"Be serious, Teddy Bear. I want to know if this is right; if it's right that I should be here with you and that we should love one another, and that it should give me electric shocks when you touch me."

"Right? Well, it's certainly good that you should have electric shocks rather than sexual repressions. Read Freud; repressions are the devil."

"Oh, you don't help me. Why aren't you ever serious? If only you knew how miserable I am sometimes, thinking it's not right. Perhaps, you know, there is a hell, and all that. I don't know what to do. Sometimes I think I ought to stop loving you."

"But could you?" asked Mr. Hutton, confident in the powers of his seduction and his moustache.

"No, Teddy Bear, you know I couldn't.

But I could run away, I could hide from you, I could lock myself up and force myself not to come to you."

"Silly little thing!" He tightened his embrace.

"Oh, dear, I hope it isn't wrong. And there are times when I don't care if it is."

Mr. Hutton was touched. He had a certain protective affection for this little creature. He laid his cheek against her hair and so, interlaced, they sat in silence, while the car, swaying and pitching a little as it hastened along, seemed to draw in the white road and the dusty hedges towards it devouringly.

"Good-bye, good-bye."

The car moved on, gathered speed, vanished round a curve, and Doris was left standing by the sign-post at the cross-roads, still dizzy and weak with the languor born of those kisses and the electrical touch of those gentle hands. She had to take a deep breath, to draw herself up deliberately, before she was strong enough to start her homeward walk. She had half a mile in which to invent the necessary lies.

Alone, Mr. Hutton suddenly found himself the prey of an appalling boredom.

II

MRS. HUTTON was lying on the sofa in her boudoir, playing Patience. In spite of the warmth of the July evening a wood fire was burning on the hearth. A black Pomeranian, extenuated by the heat and the fatigues of digestion, slept before the blaze.

"Phew! Isn't it rather hot in here?" Mr. Hutton asked as he entered the room.

"You know I have to keep warm, dear." The voice seemed breaking on the verge of tears. "I get so shivery."

"I hope you're better this evening."

"Not much, I'm afraid."

The conversation stagnated. Mr. Hutton stood leaning his back against the mantelpiece. He looked down at the Pomeranian lying at his feet, and with the toe of his right boot he rolled the little dog over and rubbed its white-flecked chest and belly. The creature lay in an inert ecstasy. Mrs. Hutton continued to play Patience. Arrived at an *impasse*, she altered the position of one card, took back another, and went on playing. Her Patiences always came out.

"Dr. Libbard thinks I ought to go to Llandrindod Wells this summer."

"Well, go, my dear—go, most certainly."

Mr. Hutton was thinking of the events of the afternoon: how they had driven, Doris and he, up to the hanging wood, had left the car to wait for them under the shade of the trees, and walked together out into the windless sunshine of the chalk down.

"I'm to drink the waters for my liver, and he thinks I ought to have massage and electric treatment, too."

Hat in hand, Doris had stalked four blue butterflies that were dancing together round a scabious flower with a motion that was like the flickering of blue fire. The blue fire burst and scattered into whirling sparks; she had given chase, laughing and shouting like a child.

"I'm sure it will do you good, my dear."

"I was wondering if you'd come with me, dear."

"But you know I'm going to Scotland at the end of the month."

Mrs. Hutton looked up at him entreatingly. " It's the journey," she said. " The thought of it is such a nightmare. I don't know if I can manage it. And you know I can't sleep in hotels. And then there's the luggage and all the worries. I can't go alone."

" But you won't be alone. You'll have your maid with you." He spoke impatiently. The sick woman was usurping the place of the healthy one. He was being dragged back from the memory of the sunlit down and the quick, laughing girl, back to this unhealthy, overheated room and its complaining occupant.

" I don't think I shall be able to go."

" But you must, my dear, if the doctor tells you to. And, besides, a change will do you good."

" I don't think so."

" But Libbard thinks so, and he knows what he's talking about."

" No, I can't face it. I'm too weak. I can't go alone." Mrs. Hutton pulled a handkerchief out of her black silk bag, and put it to her eyes.

" Nonsense, my dear, you must make the effort."

" I had rather be left in peace to die here." She was crying in earnest now.

"O Lord! Now do be reasonable. Listen now, please." Mrs. Hutton only sobbed more violently. "Oh, what is one to do?" He shrugged his shoulders and walked out of the room.

Mr. Hutton was aware that he had not behaved with proper patience; but he could not help it. Very early in his manhood he had discovered that not only did he not feel sympathy for the poor, the weak, the diseased, and deformed; he actually hated them. Once, as an undergraduate, he spent three days at a mission in the East End. He had returned, filled with a profound and ineradicable disgust. Instead of pitying, he loathed the unfortunate. It was not, he knew, a very comely emotion, and he had been ashamed of it at first. In the end he had decided that it was temperamental, inevitable, and had felt no further qualms. Emily had been healthy and beautiful when he married her. He had loved her then. But now—was it his fault that she was like this?

Mr. Hutton dined alone. Food and drink left him more benevolent than he had been before dinner. To make amends for his show of exasperation he went up to his wife's room and offered to read to her. She was touched, gratefully accepted the offer, and Mr. Hutton, who was particularly proud of his accent, suggested a little light reading in French.

"French? I am so fond of French." Mrs. Hutton spoke of the language of Racine as though it were a dish of green peas.

Mr. Hutton ran down to the library and returned with a yellow volume. He began reading. The effort of pronouncing perfectly absorbed his whole attention. But how good his accent was! The fact of its goodness seemed to improve the quality of the novel he was reading.

At the end of fifteen pages an unmistakable sound aroused him. He looked up; Mrs. Hutton had gone to sleep. He sat still for a little while, looking with a dispassionate curiosity at the sleeping face. Once it had been beautiful; once, long ago, the sight of it, the recollection of it, had moved him with an emotion profounder, perhaps, than any he had felt before or since. Now it was lined and cadaverous. The skin was stretched tightly over the cheekbones, across the bridge of the sharp, bird-like nose. The closed eyes were set in profound bone-rimmed sockets. The lamplight striking on the face from the side emphasised with light and shade its cavities and projections. It was the face of a dead Christ by Morales.

Le squelette était invisible
Au temps heureux de l'art païen.

He shivered a little, and tiptoed out of the room.

On the following day Mrs. Hutton came down to luncheon. She had had some unpleasant palpitations during the night, but she was feeling better now. Besides, she wanted to do honour to her guest. Miss Spence listened to her complaints about Llandrindod Wells, and was loud in sympathy, lavish with advice. Whatever she said was always said with intensity. She leaned forward, aimed, so to speak, like a gun, and fired her words. Bang! the charge in her soul was ignited, the words whizzed forth at the narrow barrel of her mouth. She was a machine-gun riddling her hostess with sympathy. Mr. Hutton had undergone similar bombardments, mostly of a literary or philosophic character—bombardments of Maeterlinck, of Mrs. Besant, of Bergson, of William James. To-day the missiles were medical. She talked about insomnia, she expatiated on the virtues of harmless drugs and beneficent specialists. Under the bombardment Mrs. Hutton opened out, like a flower in the sun.

Mr. Hutton looked on in silence. The spectacle of Janet Spence evoked in him an unfailing curiosity. He was not romantic enough to imagine that every face masked an interior physiognomy of beauty or strangeness, that every woman's small talk was like a vapour hanging over mysterious gulfs. His wife, for example, and Doris; they were nothing more than what they seemed to be. But with Janet Spence it was somehow different. Here one could be sure that there was some kind of a queer face behind the Gioconda smile and the Roman eyebrows. The only question was: What exactly was there? Mr. Hutton could never quite make out.

"But perhaps you won't have to go to Llandrindod after all," Miss Spence was saying. "If you get well quickly Dr. Libbard will let you off."

"I only hope so. Indeed, I do really feel rather better to-day."

Mr. Hutton felt ashamed. How much was it his own lack of sympathy that prevented her from feeling well every day? But he comforted himself by reflecting that it was only a case of feeling, not of being better. Sympathy does not mend a diseased liver or a weak heart.

"My dear, I wouldn't eat those red currants if I were you," he said, suddenly solicitous. "You know that Libbard has banned everything with skins and pips."

"But I am so fond of them," Mrs. Hutton protested, "and I feel so well to-day."

"Don't be a tyrant," said Miss Spence, looking first at him and then at his wife. "Let the poor invalid have what she fancies; it will do her good." She laid her hand on Mrs. Hutton's arm and patted it affectionately two or three times.

"Thank you, my dear." Mrs. Hutton helped herself to the stewed currants.

"Well, don't blame me if they make you ill again."

"Do I ever blame you, dear?"

"You have nothing to blame me for," Mr. Hutton answered playfully. "I am the perfect husband."

They sat in the garden after luncheon. From the island of shade under the old cypress tree they looked out across a flat expanse of lawn, in which the parterres of flowers shone with a metallic brilliance.

Mr. Hutton took a deep breath of the warm and fragrant air. "It's good to be alive," he said.

"Just to be alive," his wife echoed, stretching one pale, knot-jointed hand into the sunlight.

A maid brought the coffee; the silver pots and the little blue cups were set on a folding table near the group of chairs.

"Oh, my medicine!" exclaimed Mrs. Hutton. "Run in and fetch it, Clara, will you? The white bottle on the sideboard."

"I'll go," said Mr. Hutton. "I've got to go and fetch a cigar in any case."

He ran in towards the house. On the threshold he turned round for an instant. The maid was walking back across the lawn. His wife was sitting up in her deck-chair, engaged in opening her white parasol. Miss Spence was bending over the table, pouring out the coffee. He passed into the cool obscurity of the house.

"Do you like sugar in your coffee?" Miss Spence inquired.

"Yes, please. Give me rather a lot. I'll drink it after my medicine to take the taste away."

Mrs. Hutton leaned back in her chair, lowering the sunshade over her eyes, so as to shut out from her vision the burning sky.

Behind her, Miss Spence was making a delicate clinking among the coffee-cups.

"I've given you three large spoonfuls. That ought to take the taste away. And here comes the medicine."

Mr. Hutton had reappeared, carrying a wine-glass, half full of a pale liquid.

"It smells delicious," he said, as he handed it to his wife.

"That's only the flavouring." She drank it off at a gulp, shuddered, and made a grimace. "Ugh, it's so nasty. Give me my coffee."

Miss Spence gave her the cup; she sipped at it. "You've made it like syrup. But it's very nice, after that atrocious medicine."

At half-past three Mrs. Hutton complained that she did not feel as well as she had done, and went indoors to lie down. Her husband would have said something about the red currants, but checked himself; the triumph of an "I told you so" was too cheaply won. Instead, he was sympathetic, and gave her his arm to the house.

"A rest will do you good," he said. "By the way, I shan't be back till after dinner."

"But why? Where are you going?"

"I promised to go to Johnson's this evening. We have to discuss the war memorial, you know."

"Oh, I wish you weren't going." Mrs. Hutton was almost in tears. "Can't you stay? I don't like being alone in the house."

"But, my dear, I promised—weeks ago." It was a bother having to lie like this. "And now I must get back and look after Miss Spence."

He kissed her on the forehead and went out again into the garden. Miss Spence received him aimed and intense.

"Your wife is dreadfully ill," she fired off at him.

"I thought she cheered up so much when you came."

"That was purely nervous, purely

nervous. I was watching her closely. With a heart in that condition and her digestion wrecked—yes, wrecked—anything might happen."

"Libbard doesn't take so gloomy a view of poor Emily's health." Mr. Hutton held open the gate that led from the garden into the drive; Miss Spence's car was standing by the front door.

"Libbard is only a country doctor. You ought to see a specialist."

He could not refrain from laughing. "You have a macabre passion for specialists."

Miss Spence held up her hand in protest. "I am serious. I think poor Emily is in a very bad state. Anything might happen—at any moment."

He handed her into the car and shut the door. The chauffeur started the engine and climbed into his place, ready to drive off.

"Shall I tell him to start?" He had no desire to continue the conversation.

Miss Spence leaned forward and shot a Gioconda in his direction. "Remember, I expect you to come and see me again soon."

Mechanically he grinned, made a polite

noise, and, as the car moved forward, waved his hand. He was happy to be alone.

A few minutes afterwards Mr. Hutton himself drove away. Doris was waiting at the cross-roads. They dined together twenty miles from home, at a roadside hotel. It was one of those bad, expensive meals which are only cooked in country hotels frequented by motorists. It revolted Mr. Hutton, but Doris enjoyed it. She always enjoyed things. Mr. Hutton ordered a not very good brand of champagne. He was wishing he had spent the evening in his library.

When they started homewards Doris was a little tipsy and extremely affectionate. It was very dark inside the car, but looking forward, past the motionless form of M'Nab, they could see a bright and narrow universe of forms and colours scooped out of the night by the electric head-lamps.

It was after eleven when Mr. Hutton reached home. Dr. Libbard met him in the hall. He was a small man with delicate hands and well-formed features that were almost feminine. His brown eyes were large and melancholy. He used to waste a great deal of time sitting at the bedside of his patients, looking sadness through those eyes and talking in a sad, low voice about nothing in particular. His person exhaled a pleasing odour, decidedly antiseptic but at the same time suave and discreetly delicious.

"Libbard ?" said Mr. Hutton in surprise. "You here ? Is my wife ill ?"

"We tried to fetch you earlier," the soft, melancholy voice replied. "It was thought you were at Mr. Johnson's, but they had no news of you there."

"No, I was detained. I had a breakdown," Mr. Hutton answered irritably. It was tiresome to be caught out in a lie.

"Your wife wanted to see you urgently."

"Well, I can go now." Mr. Hutton moved towards the stairs.

Dr. Libbard laid a hand on his arm. "I am afraid it's too late."

"Too late ?" He began fumbling with his watch; it wouldn't come out of the pocket.

"Mrs. Hutton passed away half an hour ago."

The voice remained even in its softness, the melancholy of the eyes did not deepen. Dr. Libbard spoke of death as he would speak of a local cricket match. All things were equally vain and equally deplorable.

Mr. Hutton found himself thinking of Janet Spence's words. At any moment—at any moment. She had been extraordinarily right.

" What happened ? " he asked. " What was the cause ? "

Dr. Libbard explained. It was heart failure brought on by a violent attack of nausea, caused in its turn by the eating of something of an irritant nature. Red currants ? Mr. Hutton suggested. Very likely. It had been too much for the heart. There was chronic valvular disease : something had collapsed under the strain. It was all over ; she could not have suffered much.

III

"IT'S a pity they should have chosen the day of the Eton and Harrow match for the funeral," old General Grego was saying as he stood, his top hat in his hand, under the shadow of the lych gate, wiping his face with his handkerchief.

Mr. Hutton overheard the remark and with difficulty restrained a desire to inflict grievous bodily pain on the General. He would have liked to hit the old brute in the middle of his big red face. Monstrous great mulberry, spotted with meal! Was there no respect for the dead? Did nobody care? In theory he didn't much care; let the dead bury their dead. But here, at the graveside, he had found himself actually sobbing. Poor Emily, they had been pretty happy once. Now she was lying at the bottom of a seven-foot hole. And here was Grego complaining that he couldn't go to the Eton and Harrow match.

Mr. Hutton looked round at the groups

of black figures that were drifting slowly out of the churchyard towards the fleet of cabs and motors assembled in the road outside. Against the brilliant background of the July grass and flowers and foliage, they had a horribly alien and unnatural appearance. It pleased him to think that all these people would soon be dead too.

That evening Mr. Hutton sat up late in his library reading the life of Milton. There was no particular reason why he should have chosen Milton; it was the book that first came to hand, that was all. It was after midnight when he had finished. He got up from his armchair, unbolted the French windows, and stepped out on to the little paved terrace. The night was quiet and clear. Mr. Hutton looked at the stars and at the holes between them, dropped his eyes to the dim lawns and hueless flowers of the garden, and let them wander over the farther landscape, black and grey under the moon.

He began to think with a kind of confused violence. There were the stars, there was Milton. A man can be somehow the peer of stars and night. Greatness, nobility. But is there seriously a difference between the noble and the ignoble? Milton, the stars, death, and himself—himself. The soul, the body; the higher and the lower nature. Perhaps there was something in it, after all. Milton had a god on his side and righteousness. What had he? Nothing, nothing whatever. There were only Doris's little breasts. What was the point of it all? Milton, the stars, death, and Emily in her grave, Doris and himself—always himself . . .

Oh, he was a futile and disgusting being. Everything convinced him of it. It was a solemn moment. He spoke aloud: "I will, I will." The sound of his own voice in the darkness was appalling; it seemed to him that he had sworn that infernal oath which binds even the gods: "I will, I will." There had been New Year's days and solemn anniversaries in the past, when he had felt the same contritions and recorded similar resolutions. They had all thinned away, these resolutions, like smoke, into nothingness. But this was a greater moment and he had pronounced a more fearful oath. In the future it was to be different. Yes, he would live by reason, he would be industrious, he would curb his appetites, he would devote his life to some good purpose. It was resolved and it would be so.

In practice he saw himself spending his mornings in agricultural pursuits, riding round with the bailiff, seeing that his land was farmed in the best modern way —silos and artificial manures and continuous cropping, and all that. The remainder of the day should be devoted to serious study. There was that book he had been intending to write for so long—*The Effect of Diseases on Civilisation.*

Mr. Hutton went to bed humble and contrite, but with a sense that grace had entered into him. He slept for seven and a half hours, and woke to find the sun brilliantly shining. The emotions of the evening before had been transformed by a good night's rest into his customary cheerfulness. It was not until a good many seconds after his return to conscious life that he remembered his resolution, his Stygian oath. Milton and death seemed somehow different in the sunlight. As for the stars, they were not there. But the resolutions were good;

even in the daytime he could see that. He had his horse saddled after breakfast, and rode round the farm with the bailiff. After luncheon he read Thucydides on the plague at Athens. In the evening he made a few notes on malaria in Southern Italy. While he was undressing he remembered that there was a good anecdote in Skelton's jest-book about the Sweating Sickness. He would have made a note of it if only he could have found a pencil.

On the sixth morning of his new life Mr. Hutton found among his correspondence an envelope addressed in that peculiarly vulgar handwriting which he knew to be Doris's. He opened it, and began to read. She didn't know what to say; words were so inadequate. His wife dying like that, and so suddenly—it was too terrible. Mr. Hutton sighed, but his interest revived somewhat as he read on:

"Death is so frightening, I never think of it when I can help it. But when something like this happens, or when I am feeling ill or depressed, then I can't help remembering it is there so close, and I think about all the wicked things

I have done and about you and me, and I wonder what will happen, and I am so frightened. I am so lonely, Teddy Bear, and so unhappy, and I don't know what to do. I can't get rid of the idea of dying, I am so wretched and helpless without you. I didn't mean to write to you; I meant to wait till you were out of mourning and could come and see me again, but I was so lonely and miserable, Teddy Bear, I had to write. I couldn't help it. Forgive me, I want you so much; I have nobody in the world but you. You are so good and gentle and understanding; there is nobody like you. I shall never forget how good and kind you have been to me, and you are so clever and know so much, I can't understand how you ever came to pay any attention to me, I am so dull and stupid, much less like me and love me, because you do love me a little, don't you, Teddy Bear?"

Mr. Hutton was touched with shame and remorse. To be thanked like this, worshipped for having seduced the girl—it was too much. It had just been a piece of imbecile wantonness. Imbecile, idiotic:

there was no other way to describe it. For, when all was said, he had derived very little pleasure from it. Taking all things together, he had probably been more bored than amused. Once upon a time he had believed himself to be a hedonist. But to be a hedonist implies a certain process of reasoning, a deliberate choice of known pleasures, a rejection of known pains. This had been done without reason, against it. For he knew beforehand—so well, so well—that there was no interest or pleasure to be derived from these wretched affairs. And yet each time the vague itch came upon him he succumbed, involving himself once more in the old stupidity. There had been Maggie, his wife's maid, and Edith, the girl on the farm, and Mrs. Pringle, and the waitress in London, and others—there seemed to be dozens of them. It had all been so stale and boring. He knew it would be; he always knew. And yet, and yet . . . Experience doesn't teach.

Poor little Doris! He would write to her kindly, comfortingly, but he wouldn't see her again. A servant came to tell him that his horse was saddled and waiting. He mounted and rode off. That morning the old bailiff was more irritating than usual.

Five days later Doris and Mr. Hutton were sitting together on the pier at Southend ; Doris, in white muslin with pink garnishings, radiated happiness ; Mr. Hutton, legs outstretched and chair tilted, had pushed the panama back from his forehead, and was trying to feel like a tripper. That night, when Doris was asleep, breathing and warm by his side, he recaptured, in this moment of darkness and physical fatigue, the rather cosmic emotion which had possessed him that evening, not a fortnight ago, when he had made his great resolution. And so his solemn oath had already gone the way of so many other resolutions. Unreason had triumphed ; at the first itch of desire he had given way. He was hopeless, hopeless.

For a long time he lay with closed eyes, ruminating his humiliation. The girl stirred in her sleep. Mr. Hutton turned over and looked in her direction. Enough faint light crept in between the half-drawn curtains to show her bare arm and shoulder, her neck, and the dark tangle of hair on the pillow. She was beautiful, desirable. Why did he lie there moaning over his sins? What did it matter? If he were hopeless, then so be it; he would make the best of his hopelessness. A glorious sense of irresponsibility suddenly filled him. He was free, magnificently free. In a kind of exaltation he drew the girl towards him. She woke, bewildered, almost frightened under his rough kisses.

The storm of his desire subsided into a kind of serene merriment. The whole atmosphere seemed to be quivering with enormous silent laughter.

"Could anyone love you as much as I do, Teddy Bear?" The question came faintly from distant worlds of love.

"I think I know somebody who does," Mr. Hutton replied. The submarine laughter was swelling, rising, ready to break the surface of silence and resound.

"Who? Tell me. What do you mean?" The voice had come very close; charged with suspicion, anguish, indignation, it belonged to this immediate world.

"A—ah!"

"Who ?"

"You'll never guess." Mr. Hutton kept up the joke until it began to grow tedious, and then pronounced the name: "Janet Spence."

Doris was incredulous. "Miss Spence of the Manor ? That old woman ?" It was too ridiculous. Mr. Hutton laughed too.

"But it's quite true," he said. "She adores me." Oh, the vast joke! He would go and see her as soon as he returned—see and conquer. "I believe she wants to marry me," he added.

"But you wouldn't . . . you don't intend . . ."

The air was fairly crepitating with humour. Mr. Hutton laughed aloud. "I intend to marry you," he said. It seemed to him the best joke he had ever made in his life.

When Mr. Hutton left Southend he was once more a married man. It was agreed that, for the time being, the fact should be kept secret. In the autumn they would go abroad together, and the world should be informed. Meanwhile he was to go back to his own house and Doris to hers.

The day after his return he walked over in the afternoon to see Miss Spence. She received him with the old Gioconda.

"I was expecting you to come."

"I couldn't keep away," Mr. Hutton gallantly replied.

They sat in the summer-house. It was a pleasant place—a little old stucco temple bowered among dense bushes of evergreen. Miss Spence had left her mark on it by hanging up over the seat a blue-and-white Della Robbia plaque.

"I am thinking of going to Italy this autumn," said Mr. Hutton. He felt like a ginger-beer bottle, ready to pop with bubbling humorous excitement.

"Italy. . . ." Miss Spence closed her eyes ecstatically. "I feel drawn there too."

"Why not let yourself be drawn?"

"I don't know. One somehow hasn't the energy and initiative to set out alone."

"Alone. . . ." Ah, sound of guitars and throaty singing! "Yes, travelling alone isn't much fun."

Miss Spence lay back in her chair without speaking. Her eyes were still closed. Mr. Hutton stroked his moustache. The silence prolonged itself for what seemed a very long time.

Pressed to stay to dinner, Mr. Hutton did not refuse. The fun had hardly started. The table was laid in the loggia. Through its arches they looked out on to the sloping garden, to the valley below and the farther hills. Light ebbed away; the heat and silence were oppressive. A huge cloud was mounting up the sky, and there were distant breathings of thunder. The thunder drew nearer, a wind began to blow, and the first drops of rain fell. The table was cleared. Miss Spence and Mr. Hutton sat on in the growing darkness.

Miss Spence broke a long silence by saying meditatively:

"I think everyone has a right to a certain amount of happiness, don't you?"

"Most certainly." But what was she leading up to? Nobody makes generalisations about life unless they mean to talk about themselves. Happiness: he looked back on his own life, and saw a cheerful, placid existence disturbed by no great griefs or discomforts or alarms. He had always had money and freedom; he had been able to do very much as he wanted. Yes, he supposed he had been happy—happier than most men. And now he was not merely happy; he had discovered in irresponsibility the secret of gaiety. He was about to say something about his happiness when Miss Spence went on speaking.

"People like you and me have a right to be happy some time in our lives."

"Me?" said Mr. Hutton, surprised.

"Poor Henry! Fate hasn't treated either of us very well."

"Oh, well, it might have treated me worse."

"You're being cheerful. That's brave of you. But don't think I can't see behind the mask."

Miss Spence spoke louder and louder as the rain came down more and more heavily. Periodically the thunder cut across her utterances. She talked on, shouting against the noise.

"I have understood you so well and for so long."

A flash revealed her, aimed and intent, leaning towards him. Her eyes were two profound and menacing gun-barrels. The darkness re-engulfed her.

"You were a lonely soul seeking a companion soul. I could sympathise with you in your solitude. Your marriage . . ."

The thunder cut short the sentence. Miss Spence's voice became audible once more with the words :

" . . . could offer no companionship to a man of your stamp. You needed a soul mate."

A soul mate—he ! a soul mate. It was incredibly fantastic. " Georgette Leblanc, the ex-soul mate of Maurice Maeterlinck." He had seen that in the paper a few days ago. So it was thus that Janet Spence had painted him in her imagination—as a soul-mater. And for Doris he was a picture of goodness and the cleverest man in the world. And actually, really, he was what ?—Who knows ?

" My heart went out to you. I could understand ; I was lonely, too." Miss Spence laid her hand on his knee. " You were so patient." Another flash. She was still aimed, dangerously. " You never complained. But I could guess—I could guess."

" How wonderful of you ! " So he was an *âme incomprise*. " Only a woman's intuition . . ."

The thunder crashed and rumbled, died away, and only the sound of the rain was left. The thunder was his laughter, magnified, externalised. Flash and crash, there it was again, right on top of them.

"Don't you feel that you have within you something that is akin to this storm ?" He could imagine her leaning forward as she uttered the words. "Passion makes one the equal of the elements."

What was his gambit now ? Why, obviously, he should have said "Yes," and ventured on some unequivocal gesture. But Mr. Hutton suddenly took fright. The ginger beer in him had gone flat. The woman was serious—terribly serious. He was appalled.

Passion ? "No," he desperately answered. "I am without passion."

But his remark was either unheard or unheeded, for Miss Spence went on with a growing exaltation, speaking so rapidly, however, and in such a burningly intimate whisper that Mr. Hutton found it very difficult to distinguish what she was saying. She was telling him, as far as he could make out, the story of her life. The lightning was less frequent now, and there were long intervals of darkness. But at each flash he saw her still aiming towards him, still yearning forward with a terrifying intensity. Darkness, the rain, and then flash! her face was there, close at hand. A pale mask, greenish white; the large eyes, the narrow barrel of the mouth, the heavy eyebrows. Agrippina, or wasn't it rather—yes, wasn't it rather George Robey?"

He began devising absurd plans for escaping. He might suddenly jump up, pretending he had seen a burglar—Stop thief! stop thief!—and dash off into the night in pursuit. Or should he say that he felt faint, a heart attack? or that he had seen a ghost—Emily's ghost—in the garden? Absorbed in his childish plotting, he had ceased to pay any attention to Miss Spence's words. The spasmodic clutching of her hand recalled his thoughts.

"I honoured you for that, Henry," she was saying.

Honoured him for what?

"Marriage is a sacred tie, and your respect for it, even when the marriage was, as it was in your case, an unhappy one, made me respect you and admire you, and—shall I dare say the word?——"

Oh, the burglar, the ghost in the garden! But it was too late.

"... yes, love you, Henry, all the more. But we're free now, Henry."

Free? There was a movement in the dark, and she was kneeling on the floor by his chair.

"Oh, Henry, Henry, I have been unhappy too."

Her arms embraced him, and by the shaking of her body he could feel that she was sobbing. She might have been a suppliant crying for mercy.

"You mustn't, Janet," he protested. Those tears were terrible, terrible. "Not now, not now! You must be calm; you must go to bed." He patted her shoulder, then got up, disengaging himself from her embrace. He left her still crouching on the floor beside the chair on which he had been sitting.

Groping his way into the hall, and without waiting to look for his hat, he went out of the house, taking infinite pains to close the front door noiselessly behind him. The clouds had blown over, and the moon was shining from a clear sky. There were puddles all along the road, and a noise of running water rose from the gutters and ditches. Mr. Hutton splashed along, not caring if he got wet.

How heartrendingly she had sobbed! With the emotions of pity and remorse that the recollection evoked in him there was a certain resentment : why couldn't she have played the game that he was playing—the heartless, amusing game ? Yes, but he had known all the time that she wouldn't, she couldn't, play that game ; he had known and persisted.

What had she said about passion and the elements ? Something absurdly stale, but true, true. There she was, a cloud black-bosomed and charged with thunder, and he, like some absurd little Benjamin Franklin, had sent up a kite into the heart of the menace. Now he was complaining that his toy had drawn the lightning.

She was probably still kneeling by that chair in the loggia, crying.

But why hadn't he been able to keep up the game ? Why had his irresponsibility deserted him, leaving him suddenly sober in a cold world ? There were no answers to any of his questions. One idea burned steady and luminous in his mind—the idea of flight. He must get away at once.

IV

"WHAT are you thinking about, Teddy Bear?"

"Nothing."

There was a silence. Mr. Hutton remained motionless, his elbows on the parapet of the terrace, his chin in his hands, looking down over Florence. He had taken a villa on one of the hilltops to the south of the city. From a little raised terrace at the end of the garden one looked down a long fertile valley on to the town and beyond it to the bleak mass of Monte Morello and, eastward of it, to the peopled hill of Fiesole, dotted with white houses. Everything was clear and luminous in the September sunshine.

"Are you worried about anything?"

"No, thank you."

"Tell me, Teddy Bear."

"But, my dear, there's nothing to tell." Mr. Hutton turned round, smiled, and patted the girl's hand. "I think you'd better go in and have your siesta. It's too hot for you here."

"Very well, Teddy Bear. Are you coming too?"

"When I've finished my cigar."

"All right. But do hurry up and finish it, Teddy Bear." Slowly, reluctantly, she descended the steps of the terrace and walked towards the house.

Mr. Hutton continued his contemplation of Florence. He had need to be alone. It was good sometimes to escape from Doris and the restless solicitude of her passion. He had never known the pains of loving hopelessly, but he was experiencing now the pains of being loved. These last weeks had been a period of growing discomfort. Doris was always with him, like an obsession, like a guilty conscience. Yes, it was good to be alone.

He pulled an envelope out of his pocket and opened it, not without reluctance. He hated letters; they always contained something unpleasant—nowadays, since his second marriage. This was from his sister. He began skimming through the insulting home-truths of which it was composed. The words "indecent haste," "social suicide," "scarcely cold in her grave,' "person of the lower classes," all occurred. They were inevitable now in any communication from a well-meaning and right-thinking relative. Impatient, he was about to tear the stupid letter to pieces when his eye fell on a sentence at the bottom of the third page. His heart beat with uncomfortable violence as he read it. It was too monstrous! Janet Spence was going about telling everyone that he had poisoned his wife in order to marry Doris. What damnable malice! Ordinarily a man of the suavest temper, Mr. Hutton found himself trembling with rage. He took the childish satisfaction of calling names—he cursed the woman.

Then suddenly he saw the ridiculous side of the situation. The notion that he should have murdered anyone in order to marry Doris! If they only knew how miserably bored he was. Poor, dear Janet! She had tried to be malicious; she had only succeeded in being stupid.

A sound of footsteps aroused him; he looked round. In the garden below the little terrace the servant girl of the house was picking fruit. A Neapolitan, strayed somehow as far north as Florence, she was a specimen of the classical type—a little debased. Her profile might have been taken from a Sicilian coin of a bad period. Her features, carved floridly in the grand tradition, expressed an almost perfect stupidity. Her mouth was the most beautiful thing about her; the calligraphic hand of nature had richly curved it into an expression of mulish bad temper. . . . Under her hideous black clothes, Mr. Hutton divined a powerful body, firm and massive. He had looked at her before with a vague interest and curiosity. To-day the curiosity defined and focused itself into a desire. An idyll of Theocritus. Here was the woman; he, alas, was not precisely like a goatherd on the volcanic hills. He called to her.

"Armida!"

The smile with which she answered him was so provocative, attested so easy a virtue, that Mr. Hutton took fright. He was on the brink once more—on the brink. He must draw back, oh! quickly, quickly, before it was too late. The girl continued to look up at him.

"*Ha chiamato?*" she asked at last.

Stupidity or reason? Oh, there was

no choice now. It was imbecility every time.

"*Scendo*," he called back to her. Twelve steps led from the garden to the terrace. Mr. Hutton counted them. Down, down, down, down. . . . He saw a vision of himself descending from one circle of the inferno to the next—from a darkness full of wind and hail to an abyss of stinking mud.

V

FOR a good many days the Hutton case had a place on the front page of every newspaper. There had been no more popular murder trial since George Smith had temporarily eclipsed the European War by drowning in a warm bath his seventh bride. The public imagination was stirred by this tale of a murder brought to light months after the date of the crime. Here, it was felt, was one of those incidents in human life, so notable because they are so rare, which do definitely justify the ways of God to man. A wicked man had been moved by an illicit passion to kill his wife. For months he had lived in sin and fancied security—only to be dashed at last more horribly into the pit he had prepared for himself. Murder will out, and here was a case of it. The readers of the newspapers were in a position to follow every movement of the hand of God. There had been vague, but persistent, rumours in the neighbourhood; the police had taken action at last. Then came the exhumation order, the post-mortem examination, the inquest, the evidence of the experts, the verdict of the coroner's jury, the trial, the condemnation. For once Providence had done its duty, obviously, grossly, didactically, as in a melodrama. The newspapers were right in making of the case the staple intellectual food of a whole season.

Mr. Hutton's first emotion when he was summoned from Italy to give evidence at the inquest was one of indignation. It was a monstrous, a scandalous thing that the police should take such idle, malicious gossip seriously. When the inquest was over he would bring an action for malicious prosecution against the Chief Constable; he would sue the Spence woman for slander.

The inquest was opened; the astonishing evidence unrolled itself. The experts had examined the body, and had found traces of arsenic; they were of opinion that the late Mrs. Hutton had died of arsenic poisoning.

Arsenic poisoning. . . . Emily had died

of arsenic poisoning ? After that, Mr. Hutton learned with surprise that there was enough arsenicated insecticide in his greenhouses to poison an army.

It was now, quite suddenly, that he saw it : there was a case against him. Fascinated, he watched it growing, growing, like some monstrous tropical plant. It was enveloping him, surrounding him ; he was lost in a tangled forest.

When was the poison administered ? The experts agreed that it must have been swallowed eight or nine hours before death. About lunch-time ? Yes, about lunch-time. Clara, the parlour-maid, was called. Mrs. Hutton, she remembered, had asked her to go and fetch her medicine. Mr. Hutton had volunteered to go instead ; he had gone alone. Miss Spence—ah, the memory of the storm, the white aimed face ! the horror of it all !—Miss Spence confirmed Clara's statement, and added that Mr. Hutton had come back with the medicine already poured out in a wineglass, not in the bottle.

Mr. Hutton's indignation evaporated. He was dismayed, frightened. It was all too fantastic to be taken seriously, and yet this nightmare was a fact—it was actually happening.

M'Nab had seen them kissing, often. He had taken them for a drive on the day of Mrs. Hutton's death. He could see them reflected in the wind-screen, sometimes out of the tail of his eye.

The inquest was adjourned. That evening Doris went to bed with a headache. When he went to her room after dinner, Mr. Hutton found her crying.

" What's the matter ? " He sat down on the edge of her bed and began to stroke her hair. For a long time she did not answer, and he went on stroking her hair mechanically, almost unconsciously ; sometimes, even, he bent down and kissed her bare shoulder. He had his own affairs, however, to think about. What had happened ? How was it that the stupid gossip had actually come true ? Emily had died of arsenic poisoning. It was absurd, impossible. The order of things had been broken, and he was at the mercy of an irresponsibility. What had happened, what was going to happen ? He was interrupted in the midst of his thoughts.

" It's my fault—it's my fault ! " Doris

suddenly sobbed out. " I shouldn't have loved you ; I oughtn't to have let you love me. Why was I ever born ? "

Mr. Hutton didn't say anything, but looked down in silence at the abject figure of misery lying on the bed.

" If they do anything to you I shall kill myself."

She sat up, held him for a moment at arm's length, and looked at him with a kind of violence, as though she were never to see him again.

" I love you, I love you, I love you." She drew him, inert and passive, towards her, clasped him, pressed herself against him. " I didn't know you loved me as much as that, Teddy Bear. But why did you do it—why did you do it ? "

Mr. Hutton undid her clasping arms and got up. His face became very red. " You seem to take it for granted that I murdered my wife," he said. " It's really too grotesque. What do you all take me for ? A cinema hero ? " He had begun to lose his temper. All the exasperation, all the fear and bewilderment of the day, was transformed into a violent anger against her. " It's all such damned stupidity. Haven't you any conception of a civilised man's mentality? Do I look the sort of man who'd go about slaughtering people? I suppose you imagined I was so insanely in love with you that I could commit any folly. When will you women understand that one isn't insanely in love? All one asks for is a quiet life, which you won't allow one to have. I don't know what the devil ever induced me to marry you. It was all a damned stupid, practical joke. And now you go about saying I'm a murderer. I won't stand it."

Mr. Hutton stamped towards the door. He had said horrible things, he knew—odious things that he ought speedily to unsay. But he wouldn't. He closed the door behind him.

"Teddy Bear!" He turned the handle; the latch clicked into place. "Teddy Bear!" The voice that came to him through the closed door was agonised. Should he go back? He ought to go back. He touched the handle, then withdrew his fingers and quickly walked away. When he was half-way down the stairs he halted. She might try to do something silly—throw herself out of the window or God knows what! He listened attentively; there was no sound. But he pictured her very clearly, tiptoeing across the room, lifting the sash as high as it would go, leaning out into the cold night air. It was raining a little. Under the window lay the paved terrace. How far below? Twenty-five or thirty feet? Once, when he was walking along Piccadilly, a dog had jumped out of a third-storey window of the Ritz. He had seen it fall; he had heard it strike the pavement. Should he go back? He was damned if he would; he hated her.

He sat for a long time in the library. What had happened? What was happening? He turned the question over and over in his mind and could find no answer. Suppose the nightmare dreamed itself out to its horrible conclusion. Death was waiting for him. His eyes filled with tears; he wanted so passionately to live. "Just to be alive." Poor Emily had wished it too, he remembered: "Just to be alive." There were still so many places in this astonishing world unvisited, so many queer delightful people still unknown, so many lovely women never so much as seen. The huge white oxen would still be dragging their wains along the Tuscan roads, the cypresses would still go up, straight as pillars, to the blue heaven; but he would not be there to see them. And the sweet southern wines —Tear of Christ and Blood of Judas— others would drink them, not he. Others would walk down the obscure and narrow lanes between the bookshelves in the London Library, sniffing the dusty perfume of good literature, peering at strange titles, discovering unknown names, exploring the fringes of vast domains of knowledge. He would be lying in a hole in the ground. And why, why? Confusedly he felt that some extraordinary kind of justice was being done. In the past he had been wanton and imbecile and irresponsible. Now Fate was playing as wantonly, as irresponsibly, with him. It was tit for tat, and God existed after all.

He felt that he would like to pray. Forty years ago he used to kneel by his bed every evening. The nightly formula of his childhood came to him almost unsought from some long unopened chamber of the memory. "God bless Father and Mother, Tom and Cissie and the Baby, Mademoiselle and Nurse, and everyone that I love, and make me a good boy. Amen." They were all dead now—all except Cissie.

His mind seemed to soften and dissolve; a great calm descended upon his spirit. He went upstairs to ask Doris's forgiveness. He found her lying on the couch at the foot of the bed. On the floor beside her stood a blue bottle of liniment, marked "Not to be taken"; she seemed to have drunk about half of it.

"You didn't love me," was all she said when she opened her eyes to find him bending over her.

Dr. Libbard arrived in time to prevent any very serious consequences. "You mustn't do this again," he said while Mr. Hutton was out of the room.

"What's to prevent me?" she asked defiantly.

Dr. Libbard looked at her with his large, sad eyes. "There's nothing to prevent you," he said. "Only yourself and your baby. Isn't it rather bad luck on your baby, not allowing it to come into the world because you want to go out of it?"

Doris was silent for a time. "All right," she whispered. "I won't."

Mr. Hutton sat by her bedside for the rest of the night. He felt himself now to be indeed a murderer. For a time he persuaded himself that he loved this pitiable child. Dozing in his chair, he woke up, stiff and cold, to find himself drained dry, as it were, of every emotion. He had become nothing but a tired and suffering carcase. At six o'clock he undressed and went to bed for a couple of hours' sleep. In the course of the same afternoon the coroner's jury brought in a verdict of "Wilful Murder," and Mr. Hutton was committed for trial.

VI

MISS SPENCE was not at all well. She had found her public appearances in the witness-box very trying, and when it was all over she had something that was very nearly a breakdown. She slept badly, and suffered from nervous indigestion. Dr. Libbard used to call every other day. She talked to him a great deal—mostly about the Hutton case. . . . Her moral indignation was always on the boil. Wasn't it appalling to think that one had had a murderer in one's house? Wasn't it extraordinary that one could have been for so long mistaken about the man's character? (But she had had an inkling from the first.) And then the girl he had gone off with—so low class, so little better than a prostitute. The news that the second Mrs. Hutton was expecting a baby—the posthumous child of a condemned and executed criminal—revolted her; the thing was shocking—an obscenity. Dr. Libbard answered her gently and vaguely, and prescribed bromide.

One morning he interrupted her in the midst of her customary tirade. "By the way," he said in his soft, melancholy voice, "I suppose it was really you whc poisoned Mrs. Hutton."

Miss Spence stared at him for two or three seconds with enormous eyes, and then quietly said, "Yes." After that she started to cry.

"In the coffee, I suppose."

She seemed to nod assent. Dr. Libbard took out his fountain-pen, and in his neat, meticulous calligraphy wrote out a prescription for a sleeping-draught.

PERMUTATIONS AMONG THE NIGHTINGALES

PERMUTATIONS AMONG THE NIGHTINGALES

A PLAY

It is night on the terrace outside the Hotel Cimarosa. Part of the garden façade of the hotel is seen at the back of the stage—a bare white wall, with three French windows giving on to balconies about ten feet from the ground, and below them, leading from the terrace to the lounge, a double door of glass, open now, through which a yellow radiance streams out into the night. On the paved terrace stand two or three green iron tables and chairs. To the left a mass of dark foliage, ilex and cypress, in the shadow of which more tables and chairs are set. At the back to the left a strip of sky is visible between the corner of the hotel and the dark trees, blue and starry, for it is a marvellous June evening. Behind the trees the ground slopes steeply down and down to an old city in the valley below, of whose invisible presence you are made aware by the sound of many bells wafted up from a score of slender towers in a sweet and melancholy discord that seems to mourn the passing of each successive hour. When the curtain rises the terrace is almost deserted; the hotel dinner is not yet over. A single guest, COUNT ALBERTO TIRETTA, *is discovered, sitting in a position of histrionic despair at one of the little green tables. A waiter stands respectfully sympathetic at his side.* ALBERTO *is a little man with large lustrous eyes and a black moustache, about twenty-five years of age. He has the pathetic charm of an Italian street-boy with an organ—almost as pretty and sentimental as Murillo's little beggars.*

ALBERTO (*making a florid gesture with his right hand and with his left covering his eyes*). Whereupon, Waiter (*he is reciting a tale of woes*), she slammed the door in my face. (*He brings down his gesticulating right hand with a crash on to the table.*)

WAITER. In your face, Signore? Impossible!

ALBERTO. Impossible, but a fact. Some more brandy, please; I am a little weary. (*The Waiter uncorks the bottle he has been holding under his arm and fills Alberto's glass.*)

WAITER. That will be one lira twenty-five, Signore.

ALBERTO (*throwing down a note*). Keep the change.

WAITER (*bowing*). Thank you, Signore. But if I were the Signore I should beat her. (*He holds up the Cognac bottle and by way of illustration slaps its black polished flanks.*)

ALBERTO. Beat her? But I tell you I am in love with her.

WAITER. All the more reason, then, Signore. It will be not only a stern disciplinary duty, but a pleasure as well; oh, I assure you, Signore, a pleasure.

ALBERTO. Enough, enough. You sully the melancholy beauty of my thoughts. My feelings at this moment are of an unheard-of delicacy and purity. Respect them, I beg you. Some more brandy, please.

WAITER (*pouring out the brandy*). Delicacy, purity. . . . Ah, believe me, Signore . . . That will be one lira twenty-five.

ALBERTO (*throwing down another note with the same superbly aristocratic gesture*). Keep the change.

WAITER. Thank you, Signore. But as I was saying, Signore : delicacy, purity. . . . You think I do not understand such sentiments. Alas, Signore, beneath the humblest shirt-front there beats a heart. And if the Signore's sentiments are too much for him, I have a niece. Eighteen years old, and what eyes, what forms !

ALBERTO. Stop, stop. Respect my feelings, Waiter, as well as the ears of the young lady (*he points towards the glass doors*). Remember she is an American. (*The Waiter bows and goes into the hotel.*)

SIDNEY DOLPHIN *and* MISS AMY TOOMIS *come out together on to the terrace.* MISS AMY *supports a well-shaped head on one of the most graceful necks that ever issued from Minneapolis. The eyes are dark, limpid, ingenuous ; the mouth expresses sensibility. She is twenty-two and the heiress of those ill-gotten Toomis millions.* SIDNEY

DOLPHIN *has a romantic aristocratic appearance. The tailoring of* 1830 *would suit him. Balzac would have described his face as* plein de poésie. *In effect he does happen to be a poet. His two volumes of verse, "Zoetrope" and "Trembling Ears," have been recognised by intelligent critics as remarkable. How far they are poetry nobody, least of all Dolphin himself, is certain. They may be merely the ingenious products of a very cultured and elaborate brain. Mere curiosities; who knows? His age is twenty-seven.*

They sit down at one of the little iron tables. ALBERTO *they do not see; the shadow of the trees conceals him. For his part, he is too much absorbed in savouring his own despair to pay any attention to the newcomers. There is a long, uncomfortable silence.* DOLPHIN *assumes the Thinker's mask—the bent brow, the frown, the finger to the forehead.* AMY *regards this romantic gargoyle with some astonishment. Pleased with her interest in him,* DOLPHIN *racks his brains to think of some way of exploiting this curiosity to his own advantage; but he is too shy to play any of the gambits which his ingenuity suggests.* AMY *makes a social effort and speaks, in chanting Middle Western tones.*

AMY. It's been a wonderful day, hasn't it ?

DOLPHIN (*starting, as though roused from profoundest thought*). Yes, yes, it has.

AMY. You don't often get it as fine as this in England, I guess.

DOLPHIN. Not often.

AMY. Nor do we over at home.

DOLPHIN. So I should suppose. (*Silence. A spasm of anguish crosses* DOLPHIN'S *face ; then he reassumes the old Thinker's mask.* AMY *looks at him for a little longer, then, unable to suppress her growing curiosity, she says with a sudden burst of childish confidence :*)

AMY. It must be wonderful to be able to think as hard as you do, Mr. Dolphin. Or are you sad about something ?

DOLPHIN (*looks up, smiles, and blushes ; a spell has been broken*). The finger at the temple, Miss Toomis, is not the barrel of a revolver.

AMY. That means you're not specially sad about anything. Just thinking.

DOLPHIN. Just thinking.

AMY. What about ?

DOLPHIN. Oh, just life, you know—life and letters.

AMY. Letters ? Do you mean love letters.

DOLPHIN. No, no. Letters in the sense of literature ; letters as opposed to life.

AMY (*disappointed*). Oh, literature. They used to teach us literature at school. But I could never understand Emerson. What do you think about literature for ?

DOLPHIN. It interests me, you know. I read it ; I even try to write it.

AMY (*very much excited*). What, are you a writer, a poet, Mr. Dolphin ?

DOLPHIN. Alas, it is only too true ; I am.

AMY. But what do you write ?

DOLPHIN. Verse and prose, Miss Toomis. Just verse and prose.

AMY (*with enthusiasm*). Isn't that interesting ! I've never met a poet before, you know.

DOLPHIN. Fortunate being. Why, before I left England I attended a luncheon of the Poetry Union at which no less than a hundred and eighty-nine poets were present. The sight of them made me decide to go to Italy.

AMY. Will you show me your books?

DOLPHIN. Certainly not, Miss Toomis. That would ruin our friendship. I am insufferable in my writings. In them I give vent to all the horrible thoughts and impulses which I am too timid to express or put into practice in real life. Take me as you find me here, a decent specimen of a man, shy but able to talk intelligently when the layers of ice are broken, aimless, ineffective, but on the whole quite a good sort.

AMY. But I know that man already, Mr. Dolphin. I want to know the poet. Tell me what the poet is like.

DOLPHIN. He is older, Miss Toomis, than the rocks on which he sits. He is villainous. He is . . . but there, I really must stop. It was you who set me going, though. Did you do it on purpose?

AMY. Do what on purpose?

DOLPHIN. Make me talk about myself. If you want to get people to like you, you must always lead the conversation on to the subject of their characters. Nothing pleases them so much. They'll talk with enthusiasm for hours and go away saying that you're the most charming, cleverest person they've ever met. But of course you knew that already. You're Machiavellian.

AMY. Machiavellian? You're the first person that's ever said that. I always thought I was very simple and straightforward. People say about me that . . . Ah, now *I'm* talking about myself. That was unscrupulous of you. But you shouldn't have told me about the trick if you wanted it to succeed.

DOLPHIN. Yes. It was silly of me. If I hadn't, you'd have gone on talking about yourself and thought me the nicest man in the world.

AMY. I want to hear about your poetry. Are you writing any now?

DOLPHIN. I have composed the first line of a magnificent epic. But I can't get any further.

AMY. How does it go?

DOLPHIN. Like this (*he clears his throat*). "Casbeen has been, and Moghreb is no more." Ah, the transience of all sublunary things! But inspiration has stopped short there.

AMY. What exactly does it mean?

DOLPHIN. Ah, there you're asking too much, Miss Toomis. Waiter, some coffee for two.

WAITER (*who is standing in the door of the lounge*). Si, Signore. Will the lady and gentleman take it here, or in the gardens, perhaps ?

DOLPHIN. A good suggestion. Why shouldn't the lady and gentleman take it in the garden ?

AMY. Why not ?

DOLPHIN. By the fountain, then, Waiter. We can talk about ourselves there to the tune of falling waters.

AMY. And you shall recite your poetry, Mr. Dolphin. I just love poetry. Do you know Mrs. Wilcox's *Poems of Passion* ? (*They go out to the left. A nightingale utters two or three phrases of song and from far down the bells of the city jangle the three-quarters and die slowly away into the silence out of which they rose and came together.*)

(LUCREZIA GRATTAROL *has come out of the hotel just in time to overhear Miss Toomis's last remark, just in time to see her walk slowly away with a hand on* SIDNEY DOLPHIN'S *arm.* LUCREZIA *has a fine thoroughbred appearance, an aquiline nose, a finely curved sensual mouth, a superb white brow, a quivering nostril. She is the last of a family whose name is as illustrious in Venetian annals as that of Foscarini, Tiepolo, or Tron. She stamps a preposterously high-heeled foot and tosses her head.*)

LUCREZIA. Passion! Passion, indeed! An American! (*She starts to run after the retreating couple, when* ALBERTO, *who has been sitting with his head between his hands, looks up and catches sight of the newcomer.*)

ALBERTO. Lucrezia!

LUCREZIA (*starts, for in the shade beneath the trees she had not seen him*). Oh! You gave me such a fright, Alberto. I'm in a hurry now. Later on, if you . . .

ALBERTO (*in a desperate voice that breaks into a sob*). Lucrezia! You must come and talk to me. You must.

LUCREZIA. But I tell you I can't now, Alberto. Later on.

ALBERTO (*the tears streaming down his cheeks*). Now, now, now! You must come now. I am lost if you don't.

LUCREZIA (*looking indecisively first at* ALBERTO *and then along the path down which* AMY *and* SIDNEY DOLPHIN *have disappeared*). But supposing I am lost if I do come?

ALBERTO. But you couldn't be as much lost as I am. Ah, you don't know what it is to suffer. Nur wer die Sehnsucht kennt weiss wass ich leide. Oh, Lucrezia . . . (*He sobs unrestrainedly.*)

LUCREZIA (*goes over to where* ALBERTO *is sitting. She pats his shoulder and his bowed head of black curly hair*). There, there, my little Bertino. Tell me what it is. You mustn't cry. There, there.

ALBERTO (*drying his eyes and rubbing his head, like a cat, avid of caresses, against her hand*). How can I thank you enough, Lucrezia ? You are like a mother to me.

LUCREZIA. I know. That's just what's so dangerous.

ALBERTO (*lets his head fall upon her bosom*). I come to you for comfort, like a tired child, Lucrezia.

LUCREZIA. Poor darling ! (*She strokes his hair, twines its thick black tendrils round her fingers.* ALBERTO *is abjectly pathetic.*)

ALBERTO (*with closed eyes and a seraphic smile*). Ah, the suavity, the beauty of this maternal instinct !

LUCREZIA (*with a sudden access of energy and passion*). The disgustingness of it, you mean. (*She pushes him from her.*

His head wobbles once, as though it were inanimate, before he straightens into life.) The maternal instinct. Ugh! It's been the undoing of too many women. You men come with your sentimental babyishness and exploit it for your own lusts. Be a man, Bertino. Be a woman, I mean, if you can.

ALBERTO (*looking up at her with eyes full of doglike, dumb reproach*). Lucrezia! You, too? Is there nobody who cares for me? This is the unkindest cut of all. I may as well die. (*He relapses into tears.*)

LUCREZIA (*who has started to go, turns back, irresolute*). Now don't cry, Bertino. Can't you behave like a reasonable being? (*She makes as though to go again.*)

ALBERTO (*through his sobs*). You too, Lucrezia! Oh, I can't bear it, I can't bear it.

LUCREZIA (*turning back desperately*). But what do you want me to do? Why should you expect *me* to hold your hand?

ALBERTO. I thought better of you, Lucrezia. Let me go. There is nothing left for me now but death. (*He rises to his feet, takes a step or two, and then collapses into another chair, unable to move.*)

LUCREZIA (*torn between anger and remorse*).

Now do behave yourself sensibly, Bertino. There, there . . . you mustn't cry. I'm sorry if I've hurt you. (*Looking towards the left along the path taken by* AMY *and* DOLPHIN.) Oh, damnation! (*She stamps her foot.*) Here, Bertino, do pull yourself together. (*She raises him up.*) There, now you must stop crying. (*But as soon as she lets go of him his head falls back on to the iron table with an unpleasant, meaty bump. That bump is too much for* LUCREZIA. *She bends over him, strokes his head, even kisses the lustrous curls.*) Oh, forgive me, forgive me! I have been a beast. But tell me first, what's the matter, Bertino? What is it, my poor darling? Tell me.

ALBERTO. Nobody loves me.

LUCREZIA. But we're all devoted to you, Bertino mio.

ALBERTO. She isn't. To-day she shut the door in my face.

LUCREZIA. She? You mean the Frenchwoman, the one you told me about? Louise, wasn't she?

ALBERTO. Yes, the one with the golden hair.

LUCREZIA. And the white legs. I remember: you saw her bathing.

ALBERTO (*lays his hand on his heart*).

Ah, don't remind me of it. (*His face twitches convulsively.*)

LUCREZIA. And now she's gone and shut the door in your face.

ALBERTO. In my face, Lucrezia.

LUCREZIA. Poor darling!

ALBERTO. For me there is nothing now but the outer darkness.

LUCREZIA. Is the door shut for ever, then?

ALBERTO. Definitively, for ever.

LUCREZIA. But have you tried knocking? Perhaps, after all, it might be opened again, if only a crack.

ALBERTO. What, bruise my hands against the granite of her heart?

LUCREZIA. Don't be too poetical, Bertino mio. Why not try again, in any case?

ALBERTO. You give me courage.

LUCREZIA. There's no harm in trying, you know.

ALBERTO. Courage to live, to conquer. (*He beats his breast.*) I am a man again, thanks to you, Lucrezia, my inspirer, my Muse, my Egeria. How can I be sufficiently grateful. (*He kisses her.*) I am the child of your spirit. (*He kisses her again.*)

LUCREZIA. Enough, enough. I am not ambitious to be a mother, yet awhile. Quickly now, Bertino, I know you will succeed.

ALBERTO (*cramming his hat down on his head and knocking with his walking-stick on the ground*). Succeed or die, Lucrezia. (*He goes out with a loud and martial stamp.*)

LUCREZIA (*to the waiter who is passing across the stage with a coffee-pot and cups on a tray*). Have you seen the Signorina Toomis, Giuseppe ?

WAITER. The Signorina is down in the garden. So is the Signore Dolphin. By the fountain, Signorina. This is the Signore's coffee.

LUCREZIA. Have you a mother, Giuseppe ?

WAITER. Unfortunately, Signorina.

LUCREZIA. Unfortunately ? Does she treat you badly, then ?

WAITER. Like a dog, Signorina.

LUCREZIA. Ah, I should like to see your mother. I should like to ask her to give me some hints on how to bring up children.

WAITER. But surely, Signorina, you are not expecting, you—ah . . .

LUCREZIA. Only figuratively, Giuseppe. My children are spiritual children.

WAITER. Precisely, precisely! My mother, alas! is not a spiritual relation. Nor is my fiancée.

LUCREZIA. I didn't know you were engaged.

WAITER. To an angel of perdition. Believe me, Signorina, I go to my destruction in that woman—go with open eyes. There is no escape. She is what is called in the Holy Bible (*crosses himself*) a Fisher of Men.

LUCREZIA. You have remarkable connections, Giuseppe.

WAITER. I am honoured by your words, Signorina. But the coffee becomes cold. (*He hurries out to the left.*)

LUCREZIA. In the garden! By the fountain! And there's the nightingale beginning to sing in earnest! Good heavens! what may not already have happened? (*She runs out after the waiter.*)

(*Two persons emerge from the hotel, the* VICOMTE PAUL DE BARBAZANGE *and the* BARONESS KOCH DE WORMS. PAUL DE BARBAZANGE *is a young man—twenty-six perhaps—of exquisite grace. Five foot ten, well built, dark hair, sleek as marble, the most refined aristocratic features, and a monocle.* SIMONE DE WORMS *is forty, a ripe Semitic beauty. Five years more and the bursting point of overripeness will have been reached. But now, thanks to massage, powerful corsets, skin foods, and powder, she is still a beauty—a beauty of the type Italians admire, cushioned, steatopygous.* PAUL, *who has a faultless taste in bric-à-brac and women, and is by instinct and upbringing an ardent anti-Semite, finds her infinitely repulsive. The Baronne enters with a loud shrill giggle. She gives* PAUL *a slap with her green feather fan.*)

SIMONE. Oh, you naughty boy! Quelle histoire! Mon Dieu! How dare you tell me such a story!

PAUL. For you, Baronne, I would risk anything—even your displeasure.

SIMONE. Charming boy! But stories of that kind . . . And you look so innocent, too! Do you know many more like it?

PAUL (*suddenly grave*). Not of that description. But I will tell you a story of another kind, a true story, a tragic story.

SIMONE. Did I ever tell you how I saw a woman run over by a train? Cut to pieces, literally, to pieces. So disagreeable. I'll tell you later. But now, what about your story?

PAUL. Oh, it's nothing, nothing.

SIMONE. But you promised to tell it me.

PAUL. It's only a commonplace anecdote. A young man, poor but noble, with a name and a position to keep up. A few youthful follies, a mountain of debts, and no way out except the revolver. This is all dull and obvious enough. But now follows the interesting part of the story. He is about to take that way out, when he meets the woman of his dreams, the goddess, the angel, the ideal. He loves, and he must die without a word. (*He turns his face away from the Baronne, as though his emotion were too much for him, which indeed it is.*)

SIMONE. Vicomte—Paul—this young man is you?

PAUL (*solemnly*). He is.

SIMONE. And the woman?

PAUL. Oh, I can't, I mayn't tell you.

SIMONE. The woman! Tell me, Paul.

PAUL (*turning towards her and falling

on his knees). The woman, Simone, is you. Ah, but I had no right to say it.

SIMONE (*quivering with emotion*). My Paul! (*She clasps his head to her bosom. A grimace of disgust contorts Paul's classical features. He endures Simone's caresses with a stoical patience.*) But what is this about a revolver? That is only a joke, Paul, isn't it? Say it isn't true.

PAUL. Alas, Simone, too true. (*He taps his coat pocket.*) There it lies. To-morrow I have a hundred and seventy thousand francs to pay, or be dishonoured. I cannot pay the sum. A Barbazange does not survive dishonour. My ancestors were Crusaders, preux chevaliers to a man. Their code is mine. Dishonour for me is worse than death.

SIMONE. Mon Dieu, Paul, how noble you are! (*She lays her hands on his shoulder, leans back, and surveys him at arm's length, a look of pride and anxious happiness on her face.*)

PAUL (*dropping his eyes modestly*). Not at all. I was born noble, and noblesse oblige, as we say in our family. Farewell, Simone, I love you—and I must die. My last thought will be of you. (*He kisses her hand, rises to his feet, and makes as though to go.*)

SIMONE (*clutching him by the arm*). No, Paul, no. You must not, shall not, do anything rash. A hundred and seventy thousand francs, did you say? It is paltry. Is there no one who could lend or give you the money?

PAUL. Not a soul. Farewell, Simone.

SIMONE. Stay, Paul. I hardly dare to ask it of you—you with such lofty ideas of honour—but would you . . . from me?

PAUL. Take money from a woman? Ah, Simone, tempt me no more. I might do an ignoble act.

SIMONE. But from me, Paul, from me. I am not in your eyes a woman like any other woman, am I?

PAUL. It is true that my ancestors, the Crusaders, the preux chevaliers, might in all honour receive gifts from the ladies of their choice—chargers, swords, armour, or tenderer mementoes, such as gloves or garters. But money—no; who ever heard of their taking money?

SIMONE. But what would be the use of my giving you swords and horses? You could never use them. Consider, my knight, my noble Sir Paul, in these days the contests of chivalry have assumed a different form; the weapons and the armour have changed. Your sword must be of gold and paper; your breastplate of hard cash; your charger of gilt-edged securities. I offer you the shining panoply of the modern crusader. Will you accept it?

PAUL. You are eloquent, Simone. You could win over the devil himself with that angelic voice of yours. But it cannot be. Money is always money. The code is clear. I cannot accept your offer. Here is the way out. (*He takes an automatic pistol out of his pocket.*) Thank you, Simone, and good-bye. How wonderful is the love of a pure woman.

SIMONE. Paul, Paul, give that to me! (*She snatches the pistol from his hand.*) If anything were to happen to you, Paul, I should kill myself with this. You must live, you must consent to accept the money. You mustn't let your honour make a martyr of you.

PAUL (*brushing a tear from his eyes*). No, I can't. . . . Give me that pistol, I beg you.

SIMONE. For my sake, Paul.

PAUL. Oh, you make it impossible for me to act as the voices of dead ancestors tell me I should. . . . For your sake, then, Simone, I consent to live. For your sake I dare to accept the gift you offer.

SIMONE (*kissing his hand in an outburst of gratitude*). Thank you, thank you, Paul. How happy I am!

PAUL. I, too, light of my life.

SIMONE. My month's allowance arrived to-day. I have the cheque here. (*She takes it out of her corsage.*) Two hundred thousand francs. It's signed already. You can get it cashed as soon as the banks open to-morrow.

PAUL (*moved by an outburst of genuine emotion kisses indiscriminately the cheque, the Baronne, his own hands.*) My angel, you have saved me. How can I thank you? How can I love you enough? Ah, mon petit bouton de rose.

SIMONE. Oh, naughty, naughty! Not now, my Paul; you must wait till some other time.

PAUL. I burn with impatience.

SIMONE. Quelle fougue! Listen, then. In an hour's time, Paul chéri, in my boudoir; I shall be alone.

PAUL. An hour ? It is an eternity.

SIMONE (*playfully*). An hour. I won't relent. Till then, my Paul. (*She blows a kiss and runs out: the scenery trembles at her passage.*)

(PAUL *looks at the cheque, then pulls out a large silk handkerchief and wipes his neck inside his collar.*)

(DOLPHIN *drifts in from the left. He is smoking a cigarette, but he does not seem to be enjoying it.*)

PAUL. Alone ?

DOLPHIN. Alas !

PAUL. Brooding on the universe as usual ? I envy you your philosophic detachment. Personally, I find that the world is very much too much with us ; and the devil too ; (*he looks at the cheque in his hand*) and above all the flesh. My god, the flesh. . . . (*He wipes his neck again.*)

DOLPHIN. My philosophic detachment ? But it's only a mask to hide the ineffectual longings I have to achieve contact with the world.

PAUL. But surely nothing is easier. One just makes a movement and impinges on one's fellow-beings.

DOLPHIN. Not with a temperament like mine. Imagine a shyness more powerful than curiosity or desire, a paralysis of all the faculties. You are a man of the world. You were born with a forehead of brass to affront every social emergency. Ah, if you knew what a torture it is to find yourself in the presence of someone —a woman, perhaps—someone in whom you take an interest that is not merely philosophic ; to find oneself in the presence of such a person and to be incapable, yes, physically incapable, of saying a word to express your interest in her or your desire to possess her intimacy. Ah, I notice I have slipped into the feminine. Inevitably, for of course the person is always a she.

PAUL. Of course, of course. That goes without saying. But what's the trouble ? Women are so simple to deal with.

DOLPHIN. I know. Perfectly simple if one's in the right state of mind. I have found that out myself ; for moments come—alas, how rarely !—when I am filled with a spirit of confidence, possessed by some angel or devil of power. Ah, then I feel myself to be superb. I carry all before me. In those brief moments the whole secret of the world is revealed to me. I perceive that the supreme quality in the human soul is effrontery. Genius in the man of action is simply the apotheosis of charlatanism. Alexander the Great, Napoleon, Mr. Gladstone, Lloyd George—what are they ? Just ordinary human beings projected through the magic lantern of a prodigious effrontery and so magnified to a thousand times larger than life. Look at me. I am far more intelligent than any of these fabulous figures ; my sensibility is more refined than theirs ; I am morally superior to any of them. And yet, by my lack of charlatanism, I am made less than nothing. My qualities are projected through the wrong end of a telescope and the world perceives me far smaller than I really am. But the world—who cares about the world ? The only people who matter are the women.

PAUL. Very true, my dear Dolphin. The women. . . . (*He looks at the cheque and mops himself once more with his mauve silk handkerchief.*)

DOLPHIN. To-night was one of my moments of triumph. I felt myself suddenly free of all my inhibitions.

PAUL. I hope you profited by the auspicious occasion.

DOLPHIN. I did. I was making headway. I had—but I don't know why I should bore you with my confidences. Curious that one should be dumb before intimates and open one's mind to an all but stranger. I must apologise.

PAUL. But I am all attention and sympathy, my dear Dolphin. And I take it a little hardly that you should regard me as a stranger. (*He lays a hand on Dolphin's shoulder.*)

DOLPHIN. Thank you, Barbazange, thank you. Well, if you consent to be the receptacle of my woes, I shall go on pouring them out. . . . Miss Toomis . . . But tell me frankly what you think of her.

PAUL. Well . . .

DOLPHIN. A little too ingenuous, a little silly even, eh ?

PAUL. Now you say so, she certainly isn't very intellectually stimulating.

DOLPHIN. Precisely. But . . . oh, those china-blue eyes, that ingenuousness, that pathetic and enchanting silliness ! She touches lost chords in one's heart. I love the Chromatic Fantasia of Bach,

I am transported by Beethoven's hundred-and-eleventh Sonata ; but the fact doesn't prevent my being moved to tears by the last luscious waltz played by the hotel orchestra. In the best constructed brains there are always spongy surfaces that are sensitive to picture postcards and Little Nelly and the End of a Perfect Day. Miss Toomis has found out my Achilles's heel. She is boring, ridiculous, absurd to a degree, but oh ! how moving, how adorable.

PAUL. You're done for, my poor Dolphin, sunk—spurlos.

DOLPHIN. And I was getting on so well, was revelling in my new-found confidence, and, knowing its transience, was exploiting it for all I was worth. I had covered an enormous amount of ground and then, hey presto ! at a blow all my labour was undone. Actuated by what malice I don't know, la Lucrezia swoops down like a vulture, and without a by-your-leave or excuse of any kind carries off Miss Toomis from under my very eyes. What a woman ! She terrifies me. I am always running away from her.

PAUL. Which means, I suppose, that she is always pursuing you.

DOLPHIN. She has ruined my evening and, it may be, all my chances of success. My precious hour of self-confidence will be wasted (though I hope you'll not take offence at the word)—wasted on you.

PAUL. It will return.

DOLPHIN. But when—but when ? Till it does I shall be impotent and in agony.

PAUL. I know the agony of waiting. I myself was engaged to a Rumanian princess in 1916. But owing to the sad collapse in the Rumanian rate of exchange I have had to postpone our union indefinitely. It is painful, but, believe me, it can be borne. (*He looks at the cheque and then at his watch.*) There are other things which are much worse. Believe me, Dolphin, it can be borne.

DOLPHIN. I suppose it can. For, when all is said, there are damned few of us who really take things much to heart. Julie de Lespinasses are happily not common. I am even subnormal. At twenty I believed myself passionate : one does at that age. But now, when I come to consider myself candidly, I find that I am really one of those who never deeply felt nor strongly willed. Everything is profoundly indifferent to me. I sometimes try to depress myself with the thought that the world is a cesspool, that men are pathetic degenerates from the ape whose laboriously manufactured ideals are pure nonsense and find no rhyme in reality, that the whole of life is a bad joke which takes a long time coming to an end. But it really doesn't upset me. I don't care a curse. It's deplorable; one ought to care. The best people do care. Still, I must say I should like to get possession of Miss Toomis. Confound that Grattarol woman. What did she want to rush in like that for?

PAUL. I expect we shall find out now. (PAUL *jerks his head towards the left.* LUCREZIA *and* AMY *are seen entering from the garden.* LUCREZIA *holds her companion's arm and marches with a firm step towards the two men.* AMY *suffers herself to be dragged along.*)

LUCREZIA. Vicomte, Miss Toomis wants you to tell her all about Correggio.

AMY (*rather scared*). Oh, really—I . . .

LUCREZIA. And (*sternly*)—and Michelangelo. She is so much interested in art.

AMY. But please—don't trouble . . .

PAUL (*bowing gracefully*). I shall be

delighted. And in return I hope Miss Toomis will tell me all about Longfellow.

AMY (*brightening*). Oh yes, don't you just love Evangeline ?

PAUL. I do ; and with your help, Miss Toomis, I hope I shall learn to love her better.

LUCREZIA (*to* DOLPHIN, *who has been looking from* AMY *to the* VICOMTE *and back again at* AMY *with eyes that betray a certain disquietude*). You really must come and look at the moon rising over the hills, Mr. Dolphin. One sees it best from the lower terrace. Shall we go ?

DOLPHIN (*starts and shrinks*). But it's rather cold, isn't it ? I mean—I think I ought to go and write a letter.

LUCREZIA. Oh, you can do that to-morrow.

DOLPHIN. But really . . .

LUCREZIA. You've no idea how lovely the moon looks.

DOLPHIN. But I must . . .

LUCREZIA (*lays her hand on his sleeve and tows him after her, crying as she goes*). The moon, the moon. . . . (PAUL *and* AMY *regard their exit in silence.*)

PAUL. He doesn't look as though he much wanted to go and see the moon.

AMY. Perhaps he guesses what's in store for him.

PAUL (*surprised*). What, you don't mean to say you realised all the time ?

AMY. Realised what ?

PAUL. About la belle Lucrezia.

AMY. I don't know what you mean. All I know is that she means to give Mr. Dolphin a good talking to. He's so mercenary. It made me quite indignant when she told me about him. Such a schemer, too ! You know, in America we have very definite ideas about honour.

PAUL. Here too, Miss Toomis.

AMY. Not Mr. Dolphin. Oh dear, it made me so sad ; more sad than angry. I can never be grateful enough to Signorina Grattarol.

PAUL. But I'm still at a loss to know exactly what you're talking about.

AMY. And I am quite bewildered myself. Would you have believed it of him ? I thought him such a nice man.

PAUL. But what has he done ?

AMY. It's all for my money. Miss Grattarol told me. She knows. He was just asking me to marry him, and I believe I would have said Yes. But she came in just in the nick of time. It seems he only wanted to marry me because I'm so rich. He doesn't care for me at all. Miss Grattarol knows what he's like. It's awful, isn't it? Oh dear, I wouldn't have thought it of him.

PAUL. But you must forgive him, Miss Toomis. Money is a great temptation. Perhaps if you gave him another chance . . .

AMY. Impossible.

PAUL. Poor Dolphin! He's such a nice young fellow.

AMY. I thought so too. But he's false.

PAUL. Don't be too hard on him. Money probably means too much to him. It's the fault of his upbringing. No one who has not lived among the traditions of our ancient aristocracy can be expected to have that contempt, almost that hatred of wealth, which is the sign of true nobility. If he had been brought up, as I was, in an old machicolated castle on the Loire, surrounded by ancestral ghosts, imbued with the spirit of the Crusaders and preux chevaliers who had inhabited the place in the past, if he had learnt to know what noblesse oblige really means, believe me, Miss Toomis, he could never have done such a thing.

AMY. I should just think he couldn't, Monsieur de Barbazange.

PAUL. You have no idea, Miss Toomis, how difficult it is for a man of truly noble feelings to get over the fact of your great wealth. When I heard that you were the possessor of a hundred million dollars . . .

AMY. Oh, I'm afraid it's more than that. It's two hundred million.

PAUL. . . . of two hundred million dollars, then it only makes it worse; I was very melancholy, Miss Toomis. For those two hundred million dollars were a barrier, which a descendant of Crusaders and preux chevaliers could not overleap. Honour, Miss Toomis, honour forbade. Ah, if only that accursed money had not stood in the way. . . . When I first saw you—oh, how I was moved by that vision of beauty and innocence—I wanted nothing better than to stand gazing on you for ever. But then I heard about those millions. Dolphin was lucky to have felt no restraints. But enough, enough. (*He checks a rising tide of emotion.*) Give poor Dolphin another chance, Miss Toomis. At bottom he is a good fellow, and he may learn in time to esteem you for your own sake and to forget the dazzling millions.

AMY. Never. I can only marry a man who is entirely disinterested.

PAUL. But, can't you see, no disinterested man could ever bring himself to ask you? How could he prove his disinterestedness? No one would believe the purity of his intentions.

AMY (*much moved*). It is for me to judge. I know a disinterested man when I see him. Even in America we can understand honour.

PAUL (*with a sob in his voice*). Good-bye, Miss Toomis.

AMY. But no. I don't want it to be good-bye.

PAUL. It must be. Never shall it be said of a Barbazange that he hunted a woman for her money.

AMY. But what does it matter what the world says, if I say the opposite?

PAUL. You say the opposite? Thank you, thank you. But no, good-bye.

AMY. Stop. Oh! you're forcing me to do a most unwomanly thing. You're making me ask you to marry me. You're the only disinterested man I've ever met or, to judge from what I've seen of the world, I'm ever likely to meet. Haven't you kept away from me in spite of your feelings? Haven't you even tried to make me listen to another man—a man not worthy to black your boots? Oh, it's so wonderful, so noble! It's like something in a picture play. Paul, I offer myself to you. Will you take me in spite of my millions?

PAUL (*falling on his knees and kissing the hem of* AMY'S *skirt*). My angel, you're right; what does it matter what the world says as long as you believe in me? Amy, amie, bien-aimée. . . . Ah, it's too good! too, too good to be true! (*He rises to his feet and embraces her with an unfeigned enthusiasm.*)

AMY. Paul, Paul. . . . And so this is love. Isn't it wonderful? . . .

PAUL (*looking round anxiously*). You mustn't tell anyone about our engagement, my Amy. They might say unpleasant things in the hotel, you know.

AMY. Of course I won't talk about it. We'll keep our happiness to ourselves, won't we?

PAUL. Entirely to ourselves; and to-morrow we'll go to Paris and arrange about being married.

AMY. Yes, yes; we'll take the eight o'clock train.

PAUL. Not the eight o'clock, my darling. I have to go to the bank to-morrow to do a little business. We must wait till the twelve-thirty.

AMY. Very well, then. The twelve-thirty. Oh, how happy I am!

PAUL. So am I, my sweetheart. More than I can tell you. (*The sound of a window being opened is heard. They look up and see the* BARONESS *dressed in a peignoir of the tenderest blue, emerging on to the right hand of the three balconies.*)

AMY. Oh, my soul! I think I'd better go in. Good-night, my Paul. (*She runs in.*)

SIMONE. Has that horrid little American girl gone? (*She peers down; then, reassured, she blows a kiss to* PAUL.) My Romeo!

PAUL. I come, Juliet.

SIMONE. There's a kiss for you.

PAUL (*throwing kisses with both hands*). And there's one for you. And another, and another. Two hundred million kisses, my angel.

SIMONE (*giggling*). What a lot!

PAUL. It is; you're quite right. Two hundred million. . . . I come, my Juliet.

(*He darts into the hotel, pausing when just inside the door and out of sight of the* BARONESS, *to mop himself once again with his enormous handkerchief. The operation over, he advances with a resolute step. The* BARONESS *stands for a moment on the balcony. Then, seeing* DOLPHIN *and* LUCREZIA *coming in from the left, she retires, closing the window and drawing the curtains behind her.* DOLPHIN *comes striding in;* LUCREZIA *follows a little behind, looking anxiously up at him.*)

LUCREZIA. Please, please . . .

DOLPHIN. No, I won't listen to anything more. (*He walks with an agitated step up and down the stage.* LUCREZIA *stands with one hand resting on the back of a chair and the other pressed on her heart.*) Do you mean to say you deliberately went and told her that I was only after her money? Oh, it's too bad, too bad. It's infamous. And I hadn't the faintest notion that she had any money. Besides, I don't want money; I have quite enough of my own. It's infamous, infamous!

LUCREZIA. I know it was a horrible thing to do. But I couldn't help it. How could I stand by and see you being carried off by that silly little creature?

DOLPHIN. But I cared for her.

LUCREZIA. But not as I cared for you. I've got red blood in my veins ; she's got nothing but milk and water. You couldn't have been happy with her. I can give you love of a kind she could never dream of. What does she know of passion ?

DOLPHIN. Nothing, I am thankful to say. I don't want passion ; can't you understand that ? I don't possess it myself and don't like it in others. I am a man of sentimental affections, with a touch of quiet sensuality. I don't want passion, I tell you. It's too violent ; it frightens me. I couldn't possibly live with you. You'd utterly shatter my peace of mind in a day. Oh, how I wish you'd go away !

LUCREZIA. But, Sidney, Sidney, can't you understand what it is to be madly in love with somebody ? You can't be so cruel.

DOLPHIN. You didn't think much of my well-being when you interfered between Miss Toomis and me, did you ? You've probably ruined my whole life, that's all. I really don't see why you should expect me to have any pity for you.

LUCREZIA. Very well, then, I shall kill myself. (*She bursts into tears.*)

DOLPHIN. Oh, but I assure you, one doesn't kill oneself for things like that. (*He approaches her and pats her on the shoulder.*) Come, come, don't worry about it.

LUCREZIA (*throws her arms round his neck*). Oh, Sidney, Sidney . . .

DOLPHIN (*freeing himself with surprising energy and promptitude from her embrace*). No, no, none of that, I beg. Another moment and we shall be losing our heads. Personally I think I shall go to bed now. I should advise you to do the same, Miss Grattarol. You're overwrought. We might all be better for a small dose of bromide. (*He goes in.*)

LUCREZIA (*looking up and stretching forth her hands*). Sidney! . . . (DOLPHIN *does not look round, and disappears through the glass door into the hotel.* LUCREZIA *covers her face with her hands and sits for a little, sobbing silently. The nightingale sings on. Midnight sounds with an infinite melancholy from all the twenty campaniles of the city in the valley. From far away comes the spasmodic throbbing of a guitar and the singing of an Italian voice, high-pitched, passionate, throaty. The seconds pass.* LUCREZIA *rises to her feet and walks slowly into the hotel. On the threshold she encounters the* VICOMTE *coming out.*)

PAUL. You, Signorina Lucrezia? I've escaped for a breath of fresh, cool air. Mightn't we take a turn together? (LUCREZIA *shakes her head.*) Ah, well, then, good-night. You'll be glad to hear that Miss Toomis knows all about Correggio now. (*He inhales a deep breath of air. Then looking at his dinner-jacket he begins brushing at it with his hand. A lamentable figure creeps in from the left. It is* ALBERTO. *If he had a tail, it would be trailing on the ground between his legs.*)

PAUL. Hullo, Alberto. What is it? Been losing at cards?

ALBERTO. Worse than that.

PAUL. Creditors foreclosing?

ALBERTO. Much worse.

PAUL. Father ruined by imprudent speculations?

ALBERTO. No, no, no. It's nothing to do with money.

PAUL. Oh, well, then. It can't be anything very serious. It's women, I suppose.

ALBERTO. My mistress refuses to see me. I have been beating on her door for hours in vain.

PAUL. I wish we all had your luck, Bertino. Mine opens her door only too promptly. The difficulty is to get out again. Does yours use such an awful lot of this evil-smelling powder? I'm simply covered with it. Ugh! (*He brushes his coat again.*)

ALBERTO. Can't you be serious, Paul?

PAUL. Of course I can . . . about a serious matter. But you can't expect me to pull a long face about your mistress, can you, now? Do look at things in their right proportions.

ALBERTO. It's no use talking to you. You're heartless, soulless.

PAUL. What you mean, my dear Alberto, is that I'm relatively speaking bodiless. Physical passion never goes to my head. I'm always *compos mentis*. You aren't, that's all.

ALBERTO. Oh, you disgust me. I think I shall hang myself to-night.

PAUL. Do. It will give us something to talk about at lunch to-morrow.

ALBERTO. Monster! (*He goes into the hotel.* PAUL *strolls out towards the garden, whistling an air from Mozart as he goes. The window on the left opens and* LUCREZIA *steps on to her balcony. Uncoiled, her red hair falls almost to her waist. Her night-dress is always half slipping off one shoulder or the other, like those loose-bodied Restoration gowns that reveal the tight-blown charms of Kneller's Beauties. Her feet are bare. She is a marvellously romantic figure, as she stands there, leaning on the balustrade, and with eyes more sombre than night, gazing into the darkness. The nightingales, the bells, the guitar, and passionate voice strike up. Great stars palpitate in the sky. The moon has swum imperceptibly to the height of heaven. In the garden below flowers are yielding their souls into the air, censers invisible. It is too much, too much. . . . Large tears roll down* LUCREZIA'S *cheeks and fall with a splash to the ground. Suddenly, but with the noiselessness of a cat,* ALBERTO *appears, childish-looking in pink pyjamas, on the middle of the three balconies. He sees* LUCREZIA, *but she is much too deeply absorbed in thought to have noticed his coming.* ALBERTO *plants his elbows on the rail of the balcony, covers his face, and begins to sob, at first inaudibly, then in a gradual quickening crescendo. At the seventh sob* LUCREZIA *starts and becomes aware of his presence.*)

LUCREZIA. Alberto! I didn't know. . . . Have you been there long? (ALBERTO *makes no articulate reply, but his sobs keep on growing louder.*) Alberto, are you unhappy? Answer me.

ALBERTO (*with difficulty, after a pause*). Yes.

LUCREZIA. Didn't she let you in?

ALBERTO. No. (*His sobs become convulsive.*)

LUCREZIA. Poor boy!

ALBERTO (*lifting up a blubbered face to the moonlight*). I am so unhappy.

LUCREZIA. You can't be more unhappy than I am.

ALBERTO. Oh yes, I am. It's impossible to be unhappier than me.

LUCREZIA. But I *am* more unhappy.

ALBERTO. You're not. Oh, how can you be so cruel, Lucrezia? (*He covers his face once more.*)

LUCREZIA. But I only said I was unhappy, Alberto.

ALBERTO. Yes, I know. That showed you weren't thinking of me. Nobody loves me. I shall hang myself to-night with the cord of my dressing-gown.

LUCREZIA. No, no, Alberto. You mustn't do anything rash.

ALBERTO. I shall. Your cruelty has been the last straw.

LUCREZIA. I'm sorry, Bertino mio. But if you only knew how miserable I was feeling. I didn't mean to be unsympathetic. Poor boy. I'm so sorry. There, don't cry, poor darling.

ALBERTO. Oh, I knew you wouldn't desert me, Lucrezia. You've always been a mother to me. (*He stretches out his hand and seizes hers, which has gone half-way to meet him; but the balconies are too far apart to allow him to kiss it. He makes an effort and fails. He is too short in the body.*) Will you let me come on to your balcony, Lucrezia? I want to tell you how grateful I am.

LUCREZIA. But you can do that from your own balcony.

ALBERTO. Please, please, Lucrezia. You mustn't be cruel to me again. I can't bear it.

LUCREZIA. Well, then. . . . Just for a moment, but for no more. (BERTINO *climbs from one balcony to the other. One is a little reminded of the trousered monkeys on the barrel organs. Arrived, he kneels down and kisses* LUCREZIA'S *hand.*)

ALBERTO. You've saved me. You've given me a fresh desire to live and a fresh faith in life. How can I thank you enough, Lucrezia, darling?

LUCREZIA (*patting his head*). There, there. We are just two unhappy creatures. We must try and comfort one another.

ALBERTO. What a brute I am! I never thought of your unhappiness. I am so selfish. What is it, Lucrezia?

LUCREZIA. I can't tell you, Bertino; but it's very painful.

ALBERTO. Poor child, poor child. (*His kisses, which started at the hand, have mounted, by this time, some way up the arm, changing perceptibly in character as they rise. At the shoulder they have a warmth which could not have been inferred from the respectful salutes which barely touched the fingers.*) Poor darling! You've given me consolation. Now you must let me comfort your unhappiness.

LUCREZIA (*with an effort*). I think you ought to go back now, Bertino.

ALBERTO. In a minute, my darling. There, there, poor Lucrezia. (*He puts *an arm round her, kisses her hair and neck.* LUCREZIA *leans her bowed head against his chest. The sound of footsteps is heard. They both look up with scared, wide-open eyes.)*

LUCREZIA. We mustn't be seen here, Bertino. What would people think ?

ALBERTO. I'll go back.

LUCREZIA. There's no time. You must come into my room. Quickly.

(They slip through the French window, but not quickly enough to have escaped the notice of PAUL, *returning from his midnight stroll. The* VICOMTE *stands for a moment looking up at the empty balcony. He laughs softly to himself, and, throwing his cigarette away, passes through the glass door into the house. All is now silent, save for the nightingales and the distant bells. The curtain comes down for a moment to indicate the passage of several hours. It rises again with the sun.* LUCREZIA'S *window opens and she appears on the balcony. She stands a moment with one foot over the threshold of the long window in a listening pose. Then her eyes fall on the better half of a pair of*

pink pyjamas lying crumpled on the floor, like a body bereft of its soul; with her bare foot she turns it over. A little shudder plucks at her nerves, and she shakes her head as though, by this symbolic act, to shake off something clinging and contaminating. Then she steps out into the full glory of the early sun, stretching out her arms to the radiance. She bows her face into her hands, crying out loud to herself.)

LUCREZIA. Oh, why, why, why? (*The last of these Why's is caught by the* WAITER, *who has crept forth in shirt-sleeves and list-slippers, duster in hand, to clean the tables. He looks up at her admiringly, passes his tongue over his lips. Then, with a sigh, turns to dust the tables.*)

CURTAIN.

THE TILLOTSON BANQUET

THE TILLOTSON BANQUET

I

YOUNG Spode was not a snob; he was too intelligent for that, too fundamentally decent. Not a snob; but all the same he could not help feeling very well pleased at the thought that he was dining, alone and intimately, with Lord Badgery. It was a definite event in his life, a step forward, he felt, towards that final success, social, material, and literary, which he had come to London with the fixed intention of making. The conquest and capture of Badgery was an almost essential strategical move in the campaign.

Edmund, forty-seventh Baron Badgery, was a lineal descendant of that Edmund, surnamed Le Blayreau, who landed on English soil in the train of William the Conqueror. Ennobled by William Rufus, the Badgerys had been one of the very few baronial families to survive the Wars of the Roses and all the other changes and chances of English history. They were a sensible and philoprogenitive race. No Badgery had ever fought in any war, no Badgery had ever engaged in any kind of politics. They had been content to live and quietly to propagate their species in a huge machicolated Norman castle, surrounded by a triple moat, only sallying forth to cultivate their property and to collect their rents. In the eighteenth century, when life had become relatively secure, the Badgerys began to venture forth into civilised society. From boorish squires they blossomed into *grands seigneurs*, patrons of the arts, virtuosi. Their property was large, they were rich; and with the growth of industrialism their riches also grew. Villages on their estate turned into manufacturing towns, unsuspected coal was discovered beneath the surface of their barren moorlands. By the middle of the nineteenth century the Badgerys were among the richest of English noble families. The forty-seventh baron disposed of an income of at least two hundred thousand pounds a year. Following the great Badgery tradition, he had refused to have anything to do with politics or war. He occupied himself by collecting pictures; he took an interest in theatrical productions; he was the friend and patron of men of letters, of painters, and musicians. A personage, in a word, of considerable consequence in that particular world in which young Spode had elected to make his success.

Spode had only recently left the university. Simon Gollamy, the editor of the *World's Review* (the "Best of all possible Worlds"), had got to know him—he was always on the look out for youthful talent—had seen possibilities in the young man, and appointed him art critic of his paper. Gollamy liked to have young and teachable people about him. The possession of disciples flattered his vanity, and he found it easier, moreover, to run his paper with docile collaborators than with men grown obstinate and case-hardened with age. Spode had not done badly at his new job. At any rate, his articles had been intelligent enough to arouse the interest of Lord Badgery. It was, ultimately, to them that he owed the honour of sitting to-night in the dining-room of Badgery House.

Fortified by several varieties of wine and a glass of aged brandy, Spode felt more confident and at ease than he had done the whole evening. Badgery was rather a disquieting host. He had an alarming habit of changing the subject of any conversation that had lasted for more than two minutes. Spode had found it, for example, horribly mortifying when his host, cutting across what was, he prided himself, a particularly subtle and illuminating disquisition on baroque art, had turned a wandering eye about the room and asked him abruptly whether he liked parrots. He had flushed and glanced suspiciously towards him, fancying that the man was trying to be offensive. But no; Badgery's white, fleshy, Hanoverian face wore an expression of perfect good faith. There was no malice in his small greenish eyes. He evidently did genuinely want to know if Spode liked parrots. The young man swallowed his irritation and replied that he did. Badgery then told a good story about parrots. Spode was on the point of capping it with a better story, when his host began to talk about Beethoven. And so the game went on. Spode cut his conversation to suit his host's requirements. In the course of ten minutes he had made a more or less witty epigram on Benvenuto Cellini, Queen Victoria, sport, God, Stephen Phillips, and Moorish architecture. Lord Badgery thought him the most charming young man, and so intelligent.

"If you've quite finished your coffee," he said, rising to his feet as he spoke, "we'll go and look at the pictures."

Spode jumped up with alacrity, and only then realised that he had drunk just ever so little too much. He would have to be careful, talk deliberately, plant his feet consciously, one after the other.

"This house is quite cluttered up with pictures," Lord Badgery complained. "I had a whole wagon-load taken away to the country last week; but there are still far too many. My ancestors would have their portraits painted by Romney. Such a shocking artist, don't you think? Why couldn't they have chosen Gainsborough, or even Reynolds? I've had all the Romneys hung in the servants' hall now. It's such a comfort to know that one can never possibly see them again. I suppose you know all about the ancient Hittites?"

"Well . . ." the young man replied, with befitting modesty.

"Look at that, then." He indicated a large stone head which stood in a case near the dining-room door. "It's not Greek, or Egyptian, or Persian, or anything else; so if it isn't ancient Hittite, I don't know what it is. And that reminds me of that story about Lord George Sanger, the Circus King . . ." and, without giving Spode time to examine the Hittite relic, he led the way up the huge staircase, pausing every now and then in his anecdote to point out some new object of curiosity or beauty.

"I suppose you know Deburau's pantomimes?" Spode rapped out as soon as the story was over. He was in an itch to let out his information about Deburau. Badgery had given him a perfect opening with his ridiculous Sanger. "What a perfect man, isn't he? He used to . . ."

"This is my main gallery," said Lord Badgery, throwing open one leaf of a tall folding door. "I must apologise for it. It looks like a roller-skating rink." He fumbled with the electric switches and there was suddenly light—light that revealed an enormous gallery, duly receding into distance according to all the laws of perspective. "I dare say you've heard of my poor father," Lord Badgery continued. "A little insane, you know; sort of mechanical genius with a screw loose. He used to have a toy railway in this room. No end of fun he had, crawling about the floor after his trains. And all the pictures were stacked in the cellars. I can't tell you what they were like when I found them: mushrooms growing out of the Botticellis. Now I'm rather proud of this Poussin; he painted it for Scarron."

"Exquisite!" Spode exclaimed, making with his hand a gesture as though he were modelling a pure form in the air. "How splendid the onrush of those trees and leaning figures is! And the way they're caught up, as it were, and stemmed by that single godlike form opposing them with his contrary movement! And the draperies . . ."

But Lord Badgery had moved on, and was standing in front of a little fifteenth-century Virgin of carved wood.

"School of Rheims," he explained.

They "did" the gallery at high speed. Badgery never permitted his guest to halt for more than forty seconds before any work of art. Spode would have liked to spend a few moments of recollection and tranquillity in front of some of these lovely things. But it was not permitted.

The gallery done, they passed into a little room leading out of it. At the sight of what the lights revealed, Spode gasped.

"It's like something out of Balzac," he exclaimed. "Un de ces salons dorés où se déploie un luxe insolent. You know."

"My nineteenth-century chamber," Badgery explained. "The best thing of its kind, I flatter myself, outside the State Apartments at Windsor."

Spode tiptoed round the room, peering with astonishment at all the objects in glass, in gilded bronze, in china, in feathers, in embroidered and painted silk, in beads, in wax, objects of the most fantastic shapes and colours, all the queer products of a decadent tradition, with which the room was crowded. There were paintings on the walls—a Martin, a Wilkie, an early Landseer, several Ettys, a big Haydon, a slight pretty water-colour of a girl by Wainewright, the pupil of Blake and arsenic poisoner, and a score of others. But the picture which arrested Spode's attention was a medium-sized canvas representing Troilus riding into Troy among the flowers and plaudits of an admiring crowd, and oblivious (you could see from his expression) of everything but the eyes of Cressida, who looked down at him from a window, with Pandarus smiling over her shoulder.

"What an absurd and enchanting picture!" Spode exclaimed.

"Ah, you've spotted my Troilus." Lord Badgery was pleased.

"What bright harmonious colours! Like Etty's, only stronger, not so obviously pretty. And there's an energy about it that reminds one of Haydon. Only Haydon could never have done anything so impeccable in taste. Who is it by?" Spode turned to his host inquiringly.

"You were right in detecting Haydon," Lord Badgery answered. "It's by his pupil, Tillotson. I wish I could get hold of more of his work. But nobody seems to know anything about him. And he seems to have done so little."

This time it was the younger man who interrupted.

"Tillotson, Tillotson . . ." He put his hand to his forehead. A frown incongruously distorted his round, floridly curved face. "No . . . yes, I have it." He looked up triumphantly with serene and childish brows. "Tillotson, Walter Tillotson—the man's still alive."

Badgery smiled. "This picture was painted in 1846, you know."

"Well, that's all right. Say he was born in 1820, painted his masterpiece when he was twenty-six, and it's 1913 now; that's to say he's only ninety-three. Not as old as Titian yet."

"But he's not been heard of since 1860," Lord Badgery protested.

"Precisely. Your mention of his name reminded me of the discovery I made the other day when I was looking through the obituary notices in the archives of the *World's Review*. (One has to bring them up to date every year or so for fear of being caught napping if one of these old birds chooses to shuffle off suddenly.) Well there, among them—I remember my astonishment at the time—there I found Walter Tillotson's biography. Pretty full to 1860, and then a blank, except for a pencil note in the early nineteen hundreds to the effect that he had returned from the East. The obituary has never been used or added to. I draw the obvious conclusion: the old chap isn't dead yet. He's just been overlooked somehow."

"But this is extraordinary," Lord Badgery exclaimed. "You must find him, Spode—you must find him. I'll commission him to paint frescoes round this room. It's just what I've always vainly longed for—a real nineteenth-century artist to decorate this place for me. Oh, we must find him at once—at once."

Lord Badgery strode up and down in a state of great excitement.

"I can see how this room could be made quite perfect," he went on. "We'd clear away all these cases and have the whole of that wall filled by a heroic fresco of Hector and Andromache, or 'Distraining for Rent,' or Fanny Kemble as Belvidera in 'Venice Preserved'—anything like that, provided it's in the grand manner of the 'thirties and 'forties. And here I'd have a landscape with lovely receding perspectives, or else something architectural and grand in the style of Belshazzar's feast. Then we'll have this Adam fireplace taken down and replaced by something Mauro-Gothic. And on these walls I'll have mirrors, or no! let me see . . ."

He sank into meditative silence, from which he finally roused himself to shout :

" The old man, the old man ! Spode, we must find this astonishing old creature. And don't breathe a word to anybody. Tillotson shall be our secret. Oh, it's too perfect, it's incredible ! Think of the frescoes."

Lord Badgery's face had become positively animated. He had talked of a single subject for nearly a quarter of an hour.

II

THREE weeks later Lord Badgery was aroused from his usual after-luncheon somnolence by the arrival of a telegram. The message was a short one. " Found.—SPODE." A look of pleasure and intelligence made human Lord Badgery's clayey face of surfeit. " No answer," he said. The footman padded away on noiseless feet.

Lord Badgery closed his eyes and began to contemplate. Found! What a room he would have! There would be nothing like it in the world. The frescoes, the fireplace, the mirrors, the ceiling. . . . And a small, shrivelled old man clambering about the scaffolding, agile and quick like one of those whiskered little monkeys at the Zoo, painting away, painting away. . . . Fanny Kemble as Belvidera, Hector and Andromache, or why not the Duke of Clarence in the Butt, the Duke of Malmsey, the Butt of Clarence. . . . Lord Badgery was asleep.

Spode did not lag long behind his telegram. He was at Badgery House by six o'clock. His lordship was in the nineteenth-century chamber, engaged in clearing away with his own hands the bric-à-brac. Spode found him looking hot and out of breath.

"Ah, there you are," said Lord Badgery. "You see me already preparing for the great man's coming. Now you must tell me all about him."

"He's older even than I thought," said Spode. "He's ninety-seven this year. Born in 1816. Incredible, isn't it! There, I'm beginning at the wrong end."

"Begin where you like," said Badgery genially.

"I won't tell you all the incidents of the hunt. You've no idea what a job I had to run him to earth. It was like a Sherlock Holmes story, immensely elaborate, too elaborate. I shall write a book about it some day. At any rate, I found him at last."

"Where?"

"In a sort of respectable slum in Holloway, older and poorer and lonelier than you could have believed possible. I found out how it was he came to be forgotten, how he came to drop out of life in the way he did. He took it into his head, somewhere about the 'sixties, to go to Palestine to get local colour for his religious pictures—scapegoats and things, you know. Well, he went to Jerusalem and then on to Mount Lebanon and on and on, and then, somewhere in the middle of Asia Minor, he got stuck. He got stuck for about forty years."

"But what did he do all that time?"

"Oh, he painted, and started a mission, and converted three Turks, and taught the local Pashas the rudiments of English, Latin, and perspective, and God knows what else. Then, in about 1904, it seems to have occurred to him that he was getting rather old and had been away from home for rather a long time. So he made his way back to England, only to find that everyone he had known was dead, that the dealers had never heard of him and wouldn't buy his pictures, that he was simply a ridiculous old figure of fun. So he got a job as a drawing-master in a girls' school in Holloway, and there he's been ever since, growing older and older, and feebler and feebler, and blinder and deafer, and generally more gaga, until finally the school has given him the sack. He had about ten pounds in the world when I found him. He lives in a kind of black hole in a basement full of beetles. When his ten pounds are spent, I suppose he'll just quietly die there."

Badgery held up a white hand. "No more, no more. I find literature quite depressing enough. I insist that life at least shall be a little gayer. Did you tell him I wanted him to paint my room?"

"But he can't paint. He's too blind and palsied."

"Can't paint?" Badgery exclaimed in horror. "Then what's the good of the old creature?"

"Well, if you put it like that . . ." Spode began.

"I shall never have my frescoes. Ring the bell, will you?"

Spode rang.

"What right has Tillotson to go on existing if he can't paint?" went on Lord Badgery petulantly. "After all, that was his only justification for occupying a place in the sun."

"He doesn't have much sun in his basement."

The footman appeared at the door.

" Get someone to put all these things back in their places," Lord Badgery commanded, indicating with a wave of the hand the ravaged cases, the confusion of glass and china with which he had littered the floor, the pictures unhooked. " We'll go to the library, Spode; it's more comfortable there."

He led the way through the long gallery and down the stairs.

" I'm sorry old Tillotson has been such a disappointment," said Spode sympathetically.

" Let us talk about something else; he ceases to interest me."

" But don't you think we ought to do something about him? He's only got ten pounds between him and the workhouse. And if you'd seen the black-beetles in his basement!"

" Enough—enough. I'll do everything you think fitting."

" I thought we might get up a subscription amongst lovers of the arts."

" There aren't any," said Badgery.

" No; but there are plenty of people who will subscribe out of snobbism."

" Not unless you give them something for their money."

"That's true. I hadn't thought of that." Spode was silent for a moment. "We might have a dinner in his honour. The Great Tillotson Banquet. Doyen of British Art. A Link with the Past. Can't you see it in the papers? I'd make a stunt of it in the *World's Review*. That ought to bring in the snobs."

"And we'll invite a lot of artists and critics—all the ones who can't stand one another. It will be fun to see them squabbling." Badgery laughed. Then his face darkened once again. "Still," he added, "it'll be a very poor second best to my frescoes. You'll stay to dinner, of course."

"Well, since you suggest it. Thanks very much."

III

THE Tillotson Banquet was fixed to take place about three weeks later. Spode, who had charge of the arrangements, proved himself an excellent organiser. He secured the big banqueting-room at the Café Bomba, and was successful in bullying and cajoling the manager into giving fifty persons dinner at twelve shillings a head, including wine. He sent out invitations and collected subscriptions. He wrote an article on Tillotson in the *World's Review*—one of those charming, witty articles, couched in the tone of amused patronage and contempt with which one speaks of the great men of 1840. Nor did he neglect Tillotson himself. He used to go to Holloway almost every day to listen to the old man's endless stories about Asia Minor and the Great Exhibition of '51 and Benjamin Robert Haydon. He was sincerely sorry for this relic of another age.

Mr. Tillotson's room was about ten

feet below the level of the soil of South Holloway. A little grey light percolated through the area bars, forced a difficult passage through panes opaque with dirt, and spent itself, like a drop of milk that falls into an inkpot, among the inveterate shadows of the dungeon. The place was haunted by the sour smell of damp plaster and of woodwork that has begun to moulder secretly at the heart. A little miscellaneous furniture, including a bed, a washstand and chest of drawers, a table and one or two chairs, lurked in the obscure corners of the den or ventured furtively out into the open. Hither Spode now came almost every day, bringing the old man news of the progress of the banquet scheme. Every day he found Mr. Tillotson sitting in the same place under the window, bathing, as it were, in his tiny puddle of light. "The oldest man that ever wore grey hairs," Spode reflected as he looked at him. Only there were very few hairs left on that bald, unpolished head. At the sound of the visitor's knock Mr. Tillotson would turn in his chair, stare in the direction of the door with blinking, uncertain eyes. He was always full of apologies for being so slow in recognising who was there.

“ No discourtesy meant,” he would say, after asking. “ It’s not as if I had forgotten who you were. Only it’s so dark and my sight isn’t what it was.”

After that he never failed to give a little laugh, and, pointing out of the window at the area railings, would say :

“ Ah, this is the place for somebody with good sight. It’s the place for looking at ankles. It’s the grand stand.”

It was the day before the great event. Spode came as usual, and Mr. Tillotson punctually made his little joke about the ankles, and Spode as punctually laughed.

“ Well, Mr. Tillotson,” he said, after the reverberation of the joke had died away, “ to-morrow you make your re-entry into the world of art and fashion. You’ll find some changes.”

“ I’ve always had such extraordinary luck,” said Mr. Tillotson, and Spode could see by his expression that he genuinely believed it, that he had forgotten the black hole and the black-beetles and the almost exhausted ten pounds that stood between him and the workhouse. "What an amazing piece of good fortune, for instance, that you should have found me just when you did. Now, this dinner will bring me back to my place in the world. I shall have money, and in a little while—who knows? —I shall be able to see well enough to paint again. I believe my eyes are getting better, you know. Ah, the future is very rosy."

Mr. Tillotson looked up, his face puckered into a smile, and nodded his head in affirmation of his words.

"You believe in the life to come?" said Spode, and immediately flushed for shame at the cruelty of the words.

But Mr. Tillotson was in far too cheerful a mood to have caught their significance.

"Life to come," he repeated. "No, I don't believe in any of that stuff—not since 1859. The 'Origin of Species' changed my views, you know. No life to come for me, thank you! You don't remember the excitement, of course. You're very young, Mr. Spode."

"Well, I'm not so old as I was," Spode replied. "You know how middle-aged one is as a schoolboy and undergraduate.

Now I'm old enough to know I'm young."

Spode was about to develop this little paradox further, but he noticed that Mr. Tillotson had not been listening. He made a note of the gambit for use in companies that were more appreciative of the subtleties.

"You were talking about the 'Origin of Species,'" he said.

"Was I?" said Mr. Tillotson, waking from reverie.

"About its effect on your faith, Mr. Tillotson."

"To be sure, yes. It shattered my faith. But I remember a fine thing by the Poet Laureate, something about there being more faith in honest doubt, believe me, than in all the . . . all the . . . I forget exactly what; but you see the train of thought. Oh, it was a bad time for religion. I am glad my master Haydon never lived to see it. He was a man of fervour. I remember him pacing up and down his studio in Lisson Grove, singing and shouting and praying all at once. It used almost to frighten me. Oh, but he was a wonderful man, a great man. Take him for all in all, we shall not look upon his like again. As usual, the Bard is right. But it was all very long ago, before your time, Mr. Spode."

"Well, I'm not as old as I was," said Spode, in the hope of having his paradox appreciated this time. But Mr. Tillotson went on without noticing the interruption.

"It's a very, very long time. And yet, when I look back on it, it all seems but a day or two ago. Strange that each day should seem so long and that many days added together should be less than an hour. How clearly I can see old Haydon pacing up and down! Much more clearly, indeed, than I see you, Mr. Spode. The eyes of memory don't grow dim. But my sight is improving, I assure you; it's improving daily. I shall soon be able to see those ankles." He laughed, like a cracked bell—one of those little old bells, Spode fancied, that ring, with much rattling of wires, in the far-off servants' quarters of ancient houses. "And very soon," Mr. Tillotson went on, "I shall be painting again. Ah, Mr. Spode, my luck is extraordinary. I believe in it, I trust it. And after all, what is luck? Simply another name for Providence, in spite of the 'Origin of Species' and the rest of it. How right the Laureate was when he said that there was more faith in honest doubt, believe me, than in all the . . . er, the . . . er . . . well, you know. I regard you, Mr. Spode, as the emissary of Providence. Your coming marked a turning-point in my life, and the beginning, for me, of happier days. Do you know, one of the first things I shall do when my fortunes are restored will be to buy a hedgehog."

"A hedgehog, Mr. Tillotson?"

"For the blackbeetles. There's nothing like a hedgehog for beetles. It will eat blackbeetles till it's sick, till it dies of surfeit. That reminds me of the time when I told my poor great master Haydon—in joke, of course—that he ought to send in a cartoon of King John dying of a surfeit of lampreys for the frescoes in the new Houses of Parliament. As I told him, it's a most notable event in the annals of British liberty—the providential and exemplary removal of a tyrant."

Mr. Tillotson laughed again—the little bell in the deserted house; a ghostly hand pulling the cord in the drawing-room, and phantom footmen responding to the thin, flawed note.

" I remember he laughed, laughed like a bull in his old grand manner. But oh, it was a terrible blow when they rejected his designs, a terrible blow! It was the first and fundamental cause of his suicide."

Mr. Tillotson paused. There was a long silence. Spode felt strangely moved, he hardly knew why, in the presence of this man, so frail, so ancient, in body three parts dead, in the spirit so full of life and hopeful patience. He felt ashamed. What was the use of his own youth and cleverness? He saw himself suddenly as a boy with a rattle scaring birds—rattling his noisy cleverness, waving his arms in ceaseless and futile activity, never resting in his efforts to scare away the birds that were always trying to settle in his mind. And what birds! wide-winged and beautiful, all those serene thoughts and faiths and emotions that only visit minds that have humbled themselves to quiet. Those gracious visitants he was for ever using all his energies to drive away. But this old man, with his hedgehogs and his honest doubts and all the rest of it—

his mind was like a field made beautiful by the free coming and going, the unafraid alightings of a multitude of white, bright-winged creatures. He felt ashamed. But then, was it possible to alter one's life ? Wasn't it a little absurd to risk a conversion ? Spode shrugged his shoulders.

"I'll get you a hedgehog at once," he said. "They're sure to have some at Whiteley's."

Before he left that evening Spode made an alarming discovery. Mr. Tillotson did not possess a dress-suit. It was hopeless to think of getting one made at this short notice, and, besides, what an unnecessary expense!

"We shall have to borrow a suit, Mr. Tillotson. I ought to have thought of that before."

"Dear me, dear me." Mr. Tillotson was a little chagrined by this unlucky discovery. "Borrow a suit ?"

Spode hurried away for counsel to Badgery House. Lord Badgery surprisingly rose to the occasion. "Ask Boreham to come and see me," he told the footman who answered his ring.

Boreham was one of those immemorial

butlers who linger on, generation after generation, in the houses of the great. He was over eighty now, bent, dried up, shrivelled with age.

" All old men are about the same size," said Lord Badgery. It was a comforting theory. " Ah, here he is. Have you got a spare suit of evening clothes, Boreham ? "

" I have an old suit, my lord, that I stopped wearing in—let me see—was it nineteen seven or eight ? "

" That's the very thing. I should be most grateful, Boreham, if you could lend it to me for Mr. Spode here for a day."

The old man went out, and soon reappeared carrying over his arm a very old black suit. He held up the coat and trousers for inspection. In the light of day they were deplorable.

" You've no idea, sir," said Boreham deprecatingly to Spode—" you've no idea how easy things get stained with grease and gravy and what not. However careful you are, sir—however careful."

" I should imagine so." Spode was sympathetic.

" However careful, sir."

" But in artificial light they'll look all right."

"Perfectly all right," Lord Badgery repeated. "Thank you, Boreham; you shall have them back on Thursday."

"You're welcome, my lord, I'm sure." And the old man bowed and disappeared.

On the afternoon of the great day Spode carried up to Holloway a parcel containing Boreham's retired evening-suit and all the necessary appurtenances in the way of shirts and collars. Owing to the darkness and his own feeble sight Mr. Tillotson was happily unaware of the defects in the suit. He was in a state of extreme nervous agitation. It was with some difficulty that Spode could prevent him, although it was only three o'clock, from starting his toilet on the spot.

"Take it easy, Mr. Tillotson, take it easy. We needn't start till half-past seven, you know."

Spode left an hour later, and as soon as he was safely out of the room Mr. Tillotson began to prepare himself for the banquet. He lighted the gas and a couple of candles, and, blinking myopically at the image that fronted him in the tiny looking-glass that stood on his chest of drawers, he set to work, with all the ardour of a young girl preparing for her first ball. At six o'clock, when the last touches had been given, he was not unsatisfied.

He marched up and down his cellar, humming to himself the gay song which had been so popular in his middle years:

"Oh, oh, Anna Maria Jones!
Queen of the tambourine, the cymbals, and the bones!"

Spode arrived an hour later in Lord Badgery's second Rolls-Royce. Opening the door of the old man's dungeon, he stood for a moment, wide-eyed with astonishment, on the threshold. Mr. Tillotson was standing by the empty grate, one elbow resting on the mantelpiece, one leg crossed over the other in a jaunty and gentlemanly attitude. The effect of the candlelight shining on his face was to deepen every line and wrinkle with intense black shadow; he looked immeasurably old. It was a noble and pathetic head. On the other hand, Boreham's outworn evening-suit was simply buffoonish. The coat was too long in the sleeves and the tail; the trousers bagged in elephantine creases about his ankles. Some of the grease-spots were visible even in candlelight. The white tie, over which Mr. Tillotson had taken infinite pains and which he believed in his purblindness to be perfect, was fantastically lop-sided. He had buttoned up his waistcoat in such a fashion that one button was widowed of its hole and one hole of its button. Across his shirt front lay the broad green ribbon of some unknown Order.

"Queen of the tambourine, the cymbals, and the bones," Mr. Tillotson concluded in a gnat-like voice before welcoming his visitor.

"Well, Spode, here you are. I'm dressed already, you see. The suit, I flatter myself, fits very well, almost as though it had been made for me. I am all gratitude to the gentleman who was kind enough to lend it to me; I shall take the greatest care of it. It's a dangerous thing to lend clothes. For loan oft loseth both itself and friend. The Bard is always right."

"Just one thing," said Spode. "A touch to your waistcoat." He unbuttoned the dissipated garment and did it up again more symmetrically.

Mr. Tillotson was a little piqued at being found so absurdly in the wrong.

"Thanks, thanks," he said protestingly, trying to edge away from his valet. "It's all right, you know; I can do it myself. Foolish oversight. I flatter myself the suit fits very well."

"And perhaps the tie might . . ." Spode began tentatively. But the old man would not hear of it.

"No, no. The tie's all right. I can tie a tie, Mr. Spode. The tie's all right. Leave it as it is, I beg."

"I like your Order."

Mr. Tillotson looked down complacently at his shirt front. "Ah, you've noticed my Order. It's a long time since I wore that. It was given me by the Grand Porte, you know, for services rendered in the Russo-Turkish War. It's the Order of Chastity, the second class. They only give the first class to crowned heads, you know—crowned heads and ambassadors. And only Pashas of the highest rank get the second. Mine's the second. They only give the first class to crowned heads . . ."

"Of course, of course," said Spode.

"Do you think I look all right, Mr. Spode?" Mr. Tillotson asked, a little anxiously.

"Splendid, Mr. Tillotson—splendid. The Order's magnificent."

The old man's face brightened once more. "I flatter myself," he said, "that this borrowed suit fits me very well. But I don't like borrowing clothes. For loan oft loseth both itself and friend, you know. And the Bard is always right."

"Ugh, there's one of those horrible beetles!" Spode exclaimed.

Mr. Tillotson bent down and stared at the floor. "I see it," he said, and stamped on a small piece of coal, which crunched to powder under his foot. "I shall certainly buy a hedgehog."

It was time for them to start. A crowd of little boys and girls had collected round Lord Badgery's enormous car. The chauffeur, who felt that honour and dignity were at stake, pretended not to notice the children, but sat gazing, like a statue, into eternity. At the sight of Spode and Mr. Tillotson emerging from the house a yell of mingled awe and derision went up. It subsided to an astonished silence as they climbed into the car. "Bomba's," Spode directed. The Rolls-Royce gave a faintly stertorous sigh and began to move. The children yelled again, and ran along beside the car, waving their arms in a frenzy of excitement. It was then that Mr. Tillotson, with an incomparably noble gesture, leaned forward and tossed among the seething crowd of urchins his three last coppers.

IV

IN Bomba's big room the company was assembling. The long gilt-edged mirrors reflected a singular collection of people. Middle-aged Academicians shot suspicious glances at youths whom they suspected, only too correctly, of being iconoclasts, organisers of Post-Impressionist Exhibitions. Rival art critics, brought suddenly face to face, quivered with restrained hatred. Mrs. Nobes, Mrs. Cayman, and Mrs. Mandragore, those indefatigable hunters of artistic big game, came on one another all unawares in this well-stored menagerie, where each had expected to hunt alone, and were filled with rage. Through this crowd of mutually repellent vanities Lord Badgery moved with a suavity that seemed unconscious of all the feuds and hatreds. He was enjoying himself immensely. Behind the heavy waxen mask of his face, ambushed behind the Hanoverian nose, the little lustreless pig's eyes, the pale thick lips, there lurked a small devil of happy malice that rocked with laughter.

" So nice of you to have come, Mrs. Mandragore, to do honour to England's artistic past. And I'm so glad to see you've brought dear Mrs. Cayman. And is that Mrs. Nobes, too? So it is! I hadn't noticed her before. How delightful! I knew we could depend on your love of art."

And he hurried away to seize the opportunity of introducing that eminent sculptor, Sir Herbert Herne, to the bright young critic who had called him, in the public prints, a monumental mason.

A moment later the Maître d'Hôtel came to the door of the gilded saloon and announced, loudly and impressively, " Mr. Walter Tillotson." Guided from behind by young Spode, Mr. Tillotson came into the room slowly and hesitatingly. In the glare of the lights his eyelids beat heavily, painfully, like the wings of an imprisoned moth, over his filmy eyes. Once inside the door he halted and drew himself up with a conscious assumption of dignity. Lord Badgery hurried forward and seized his hand.

"Welcome, Mr. Tillotson—welcome in the name of English art!"

Mr. Tillotson inclined his head in silence. He was too full of emotion to be able to reply.

"I should like to introduce you to a few of your younger colleagues, who have assembled here to do you honour."

Lord Badgery presented everyone in the room to the old painter, who bowed, shook hands, made little noises in his throat, but still found himself unable to speak. Mrs. Nobes, Mrs. Cayman, and Mrs. Mandragore all said charming things.

Dinner was served; the party took their places. Lord Badgery sat at the head of the table, with Mr. Tillotson on his right hand and Sir Herbert Herne on his left. Confronted with Bomba's succulent cooking and Bomba's wines, Mr. Tillotson ate and drank a good deal. He had the appetite of one who has lived on greens and potatoes for ten years among the blackbeetles. After the second glass of wine he began to talk, suddenly and in a flood, as though a sluice had been pulled up.

"In Asia Minor," he began, "it is the custom, when one goes to dinner, to hiccough as a sign of appreciative fullness. *Eructavit cor meum*, as the Psalmist has it; he was an Oriental himself."

Spode had arranged to sit next to Mrs. Cayman; he had designs upon her. She was an impossible woman, of course, but rich and useful; he wanted to bamboozle her into buying some of his young friends' pictures.

"In a cellar?" Mrs. Cayman was saying, "with blackbeetles? Oh, how dreadful! Poor old man! And he's ninety-seven, didn't you say? Isn't that shocking! I only hope the subscription will be a large one. Of course, one wishes one could have given more oneself. But then, you know, one has so many expenses, and things are so difficult now."

"I know, I know," said Spode, with feeling.

"It's all because of Labour," Mrs. Cayman explained. "Of course, I should simply love to have him in to dinner sometimes. But, then, I feel he's really too old, too *farouche* and *gâteux*; it would not be doing a kindness to him, would it? And so you are working with Mr. Gollamy now? What a charming man, so talented, such conversation . . ."

"*Eructavit cor meum*," said Mr. Tillotson for the third time. Lord Badgery tried to head him off the subject of Turkish etiquette, but in vain.

By half-past nine a kinder vinolent atmosphere had put to sleep the hatreds and suspicions of before dinner. Sir Herbert Herne had discovered that the young Cubist sitting next him was not insane and actually knew a surprising amount about the Old Masters. For their part these young men had realised that their elders were not at all malignant; they were just very stupid and pathetic. It was only in the bosoms of Mrs. Nobes, Mrs. Cayman, and Mrs. Mandragore that hatred still reigned undiminished. Being ladies and old-fashioned, they had drunk almost no wine.

The moment for speech-making arrived. Lord Badgery rose to his feet, said what was expected of him, and called upon Sir Herbert to propose the toast of the evening. Sir Herbert coughed, smiled, and began. In the course of a speech that lasted twenty minutes he told anecdotes of Mr. Gladstone, Lord Leighton, Sir Alma Tadema, and the late Bishop of Bombay; he made three puns, he quoted

Shakespeare and Whittier, he was playful, he was eloquent, he was grave. . . . At the end of his harangue Sir Herbert handed to Mr. Tillotson a silk purse containing fifty-eight pounds ten shillings, the total amount of the subscription. The old man's health was drunk with acclamation.

Mr. Tillotson rose with difficulty to his feet. The dry, snakelike skin of his face was flushed; his tie was more crooked than ever; the green ribbon of the Order of Chastity of the second class had somehow climbed up his crumpled and maculate shirt-front.

"My lords, ladies, and gentlemen," he began in a choking voice, and then broke down completely. It was a very painful and pathetic spectacle. A feeling of intense discomfort afflicted the minds of all who looked upon that trembling relic of a man, as he stood there weeping and stammering. It was as though a breath of the wind of death had blown suddenly through the room, lifting the vapours of wine and tobacco-smoke, quenching the laughter and the candle flames. Eyes floated uneasily, not knowing where to look. Lord Badgery, with great presence of mind, offered the old man a glass of wine. Mr. Tillotson began to recover. The guests heard him murmur a few disconnected words.

"This great honour . . . overwhelmed with kindness . . . this magnificent banquet . . . not used to it . . . in Asia Minor . . . *eructavit cor meum.*"

At this point Lord Badgery plucked sharply at one of his long coat tails. Mr. Tillotson paused, took another sip of wine, and then went on with a newly won coherence and energy.

"The life of the artist is a hard one. His work is unlike other men's work, which may be done mechanically, by rote and almost, as it were, in sleep. It demands from him a constant expense of spirit. He gives continually of his best life, and in return he receives much joy, it is true—much fame, it may be—but of material blessings, very few. It is eighty years since first I devoted my life to the service of art; eighty years, and almost every one of those years has brought me fresh and painful proof of what I have been saying: the artist's life is a hard one."

This unexpected deviation into sense increased the general feeling of discomfort. It became necessary to take the old man seriously, to regard him as a human being. Up till then he had been no more than an object of curiosity, a mummy in an absurd suit of evening-clothes with a green ribbon across the shirt front. People could not help wishing that they had subscribed a little more. Fifty-eight pounds ten—it wasn't enormous. But happily for the peace of mind of the company, Mr. Tillotson paused again, took another sip of wine, and began to live up to his proper character by talking absurdly.

"When I consider the life of that great man, Benjamin Robert Haydon, one of the greatest men England has ever produced . . ." The audience heaved a sigh of relief; this was all as it should be. There was a burst of loud bravoing and clapping. Mr. Tillotson turned his dim eyes round the room, and smiled gratefully at the misty figures he beheld. "That great man, Benjamin Robert Haydon," he continued, "whom I am proud to call my master and who, it rejoices my heart to see, still lives in your memory and esteem,—that great man, one of the greatest that England has ever produced, led a life so deplorable that I cannot think of it without a tear."

And with infinite repetitions and divagations, Mr. Tillotson related the history of B. R. Haydon, his imprisonments for debt, his battle with the Academy, his triumphs, his failures, his despair, his suicide. Half-past ten struck. Mr. Tillotson was declaiming against the stupid and prejudiced judges who had rejected Haydon's designs for the decoration of the new Houses of Parliament in favour of the paltriest German scribblings.

"That great man, one of the greatest England has ever produced, that great Benjamin Robert Haydon, whom I am proud to call my master and who, it rejoices me to see, still lives on in your memory and esteem—at that affront his great heart burst; it was the unkindest cut of all. He who had worked all his life for the recognition of the artist by the State, he who had petitioned every Prime Minister, including the Duke of Wellington, for thirty years, begging them to employ artists to decorate public buildings, he to whom the scheme for decorating the Houses of Parliament was undeniably due . . ." Mr. Tillotson lost a grip on his syntax and began a new sentence. "It was the unkindest cut of all, it was the last straw. The artist's life is a hard one."

At eleven Mr. Tillotson was talking about the pre-Raphaelites. At a quarter-past he had begun to tell the story of B. R. Haydon all over again. At twenty-five minutes to twelve he collapsed quite speechless into his chair. Most of the guests had already gone away; the few who remained made haste to depart. Lord Badgery led the old man to the door and packed him into the second Rolls-Royce. The Tillotson Banquet was over; it had been a pleasant evening, but a little too long.

Spode walked back to his rooms in Bloomsbury, whistling as he went. The arc lamps of Oxford Street reflected in the polished surface of the road: canals of dark bronze. He would have to bring that into an article some time. The Cayman woman had been very successfully nobbled. "Voi che sapete," he whistled—somewhat out of tune, but he could not hear that.

When Mr. Tillotson's landlady came in to call him on the following morning, she found the old man lying fully dressed on his bed. He looked very ill and very, very old; Boreham's dress-suit was in a terrible state, and the green ribbon of the Order of Chastity was ruined. Mr. Tillotson lay very still, but he was not asleep. Hearing the sound of footsteps, he opened his eyes a little and faintly groaned. His landlady looked down at him menacingly.

"Disgusting!" she said; "disgusting, I call it. At your age."

Mr. Tillotson groaned again. Making a great effort, he drew out of his trouser pocket a large silk purse, opened it, and extracted a sovereign.

"The artist's life is a hard one, Mrs. Green," he said, handing her the coin. "Would you mind sending for the doctor? I don't feel very well. And oh, what shall I do about these clothes? What shall I say to the gentleman who was kind enough to lend them to me? Loan oft loseth both itself and friend. The Bard is always right."

GREEN TUNNELS

GREEN TUNNELS

"IN the Italian gardens of the thirteenth century . . ." Mr. Buzzacott interrupted himself to take another helping of the risotto which was being offered him. "Excellent risotto this," he observed. "Nobody who was not born in Milan can make it properly. So they say."

"So they say," Mr. Topes repeated in his sad, apologetic voice, and helped himself in his turn.

"Personally," said Mrs. Topes, with decision, "I find all Italian cooking abominable. I don't like the oil—especially hot. No, thank you." She recoiled from the proffered dish.

After the first mouthful Mr. Buzzacott put down his fork. "In the Italian gardens of the thirteenth century," he began again, making with his long, pale hand a curved and flowery gesture that ended with a clutch at his beard, "a frequent and most felicitous use was made of green tunnels."

"Green tunnels?" Barbara woke up suddenly from her tranced silence. "Green tunnels?"

"Yes, my dear," said her father. "Green tunnels. Arched alleys covered with vines or other creeping plants. Their length was often very considerable."

But Barbara had once more ceased to pay attention to what he was saying. Green tunnels—the words had floated down to her, through profound depths of reverie, across great spaces of abstraction, startling her like the sound of a strange-voiced bell. Green tunnels—what a wonderful idea. She would not listen to her father explaining the phrase into dullness. He made everything dull; an inverted alchemist, turning gold into lead. She pictured caverns in a great aquarium, long vistas between rocks and scarcely swaying weeds and pale, discoloured corals; endless dim green corridors with huge lazy fishes loitering aimlessly along them. Green-faced monsters with goggling eyes and mouths that slowly opened and shut. Green tunnels . . .

"I have seen them illustrated in illuminated manuscripts of the period," Mr. Buzzacott went on; once more he clutched his pointed brown beard—clutched and combed it with his long fingers.

Mr. Topes looked up. The glasses of his round owlish spectacles flashed as he moved his head. "I know what you mean," he said.

"I have a very good mind to have one planted in my garden here."

"It will take a long time to grow," said Mr. Topes. "In this sand, so close to the sea, you will only be able to plant vines. And they come up very slowly—very slowly indeed." He shook his head, and the points of light danced wildly in his spectacles. His voice drooped hopelessly, his grey moustache drooped, his whole person drooped. Then, suddenly, he pulled himself up. A shy, apologetic smile appeared on his face. He wriggled uncomfortably. Then, with a final rapid shake of the head, he gave vent to a quotation:

> "But at my back I always hear
> Time's winged chariot hurrying near."

He spoke deliberately, and his voice trembled a little. He always found it painfully difficult to say something choice and out of the ordinary; and yet what a wealth of remembered phrase, what apt new coinages were always surging through his mind!

"They don't grow so slowly as all that," said Mr. Buzzacott confidently. He was only just over fifty, and looked a handsome thirty-five. He gave himself at least another forty years; indeed, he had not yet begun to contemplate the possibility of ever concluding.

"Miss Barbara will enjoy it, perhaps—your green tunnel." Mr. Topes sighed and looked across the table at his host's daughter.

Barbara was sitting with her elbows on the table, her chin in her hands, staring in front of her. The sound of her own name reached her faintly. She turned her head in Mr. Topes's direction and found herself confronted by the glitter of his round, convex spectacles. At the end of the green tunnel—she stared at the shining circles—hung the eyes of a goggling fish. They approached, floating, closer and closer, along the dim submarine corridor.

Confronted by this fixed regard, Mr. Topes looked away. What thoughtful eyes! He couldn't remember ever to have seen eyes so full of thought. There were certain Madonnas of Montagna, he reflected, very like her: mild little blonde Madonnas with slightly snub noses and very, very young. But he was old; it would be many years, in spite of Buzzacott, before the vines grew up into a green tunnel. He took a sip of wine; then, mechanically, sucked his drooping grey moustache.

"Arthur!"

At the sound of his wife's voice Mr. Topes started, raised his napkin to his mouth. Mrs. Topes did not permit the sucking of moustaches. It was only in moments of absent-mindedness that he ever offended, now.

"The Marchese Prampolini is coming here to take coffee," said Mr. Buzzacott suddenly. "I almost forgot to tell you."

"One of these Italian marquises, I suppose," said Mrs. Topes, who was no snob, except in England. She raised her chin with a little jerk.

Mr. Buzzacott executed an upward curve of the hand in her direction. "I assure you, Mrs. Topes, he belongs to a very old and distinguished family. They are Genoese in origin. You remember their palace, Barbara ? Built by Alessi."

Barbara looked up. "Oh yes," she said vaguely. "Alessi. I know." Alessi: Aleppo—where a malignant and a turbaned Turk. *And* a turbaned ; that had always seemed to her very funny.

"Several of his ancestors," Mr. Buzzacott went on, "distinguished themselves as viceroys of Corsica. They did good work in the suppression of rebellion. Strange, isn't it"—he turned parenthetically to Mr. Topes—"the way in which sympathy is always on the side of rebels ? What a fuss people made of Corsica! That ridiculous book by Gregorovius, for example. And the Irish, and the Poles, and all the rest of them. It always seems to me very superfluous and absurd."

"Isn't it, perhaps, a little natural ?" Mr. Topes began timorously and tentatively; but his host went on without listening.

"The present marquis," he said, "is the head of the local Fascisti. They have done no end of good work in this district in the way of preserving law and order and keeping the lower classes in their place."

"Ah, the Fascisti," Mrs. Topes repeated approvingly. "One would like to see something of the kind in England. What with all these strikes . . ."

"He has asked me for a subscription to the funds of the organisation. I shall give him one, of course."

"Of course." Mrs. Topes nodded. "My nephew, the one who was a major during the war, volunteered in the last coal strike. He was sorry, I know, that it didn't come to a fight. 'Aunt Annie,' he said to me, when I saw him last, 'if there had been a fight we should have knocked them out completely — completely.'"

In Aleppo, the Fascisti, malignant *and* turbaned, were fighting, under the palm trees. Weren't they palm trees, those tufted green plumes?

"What, no ice to-day? *Niente gelato*?" inquired Mr. Buzzacott as the maid put down the compote of peaches on the table.

Concetta apologised. The ice-making machine in the village had broken down. There would be no ice till to-morrow.

"Too bad," said Mr. Buzzacott. "*Troppo male, Concetta.*"

Under the palm trees, Barbara saw them: they pranced about, fighting. They were mounted on big dogs, and in the trees were enormous many-coloured birds.

"Goodness me, the child's asleep." Mrs. Topes was proffering the dish of peaches. "How much longer am I to hold this in front of your nose, Barbara?"

Barbara felt herself blushing. "I'm so sorry," she mumbled, and took the dish clumsily.

"Day-dreaming. It's a bad habit."

"It's one we all succumb to sometimes," put in Mr. Topes deprecatingly, with a little nervous tremble of the head.

"You may, my dear," said his wife. "I do not."

Mr. Topes lowered his eyes to his plate and went on eating.

"The *marchese* should be here at any moment now," said Mr. Buzzacott, looking at his watch. "I hope he won't be late. I find I suffer so much from any postponement of my siesta. This Italian heat," he added, with growing plaintiveness, "one can't be too careful."

"Ah, but when I was with my father in India," began Mrs. Topes in a tone of superiority: "he was an Indian civilian, you know . . ."

Aleppo, India—always the palm trees. Cavalcades of big dogs, and tigers too.

Concetta ushered in the marquis. Delighted. Pleased to meet. Speak English? Yés, yéss. *Pocchino*. Mrs. Topes: and Mr. Topes, the distinguished antiquarian. Ah, of course; know his name very well. My daughter. Charmed. Often seen the signorina bathing. Admired the way she dives. Beautiful—the hand made a long, caressing gesture. These athletic English signorine. The teeth flashed astonishingly white in the brown face, the dark eyes glittered. She felt herself blushing again, looked away, smiled foolishly. The marquis had already turned back to Mr. Buzzacott.

"So you have decided to settle in our Carrarese."

Well, not settled exactly; Mr. Buzzacott wouldn't go so far as to say settled. A villino for the summer months. The winter in Rome. One was forced to live abroad. Taxation in England. . . . Soon they were all talking. Barbara looked at them. Beside the marquis they all seemed half dead. His face flashed as he talked; he seemed to be boiling with life. Her father was limp and pale, like something long buried from the light; and Mr. Topes was all dry and shrivelled; and Mrs. Topes looked more than ever like something worked by clockwork. They were talking about Socialism and Fascisti, and all that. Barbara did not listen to what they were saying; but she looked at them, absorbed.

Good-bye, good-bye. The animated face with its flash of a smile was turned like a lamp from one to another. Now it was turned on her. Perhaps one evening she would come, with her father, and the Signora Topes. He and his sister gave little dances sometimes. Only the gramophone, of course. But that was better than nothing, and the signorina must dance divinely—another flash—he could see that. He pressed her hand again. Good-bye.

It was time for the siesta.

"Don't forget to pull down the mosquito netting, my dear," Mr. Buzzacott exhorted. "There is always a danger of anophylines."

"All right, father." She moved towards the door without turning round to answer him. He was always terribly tiresome about mosquito nets. Once they had driven through the Campagna in a hired cab, completely enclosed in an improvised tent of netting. The monuments along the Appian Way had loomed up mistily as through bridal veils. And how everyone had laughed. But her father, of course, hadn't so much as noticed it. He never noticed anything.

"Is it at Berlin, that charming little Madonna of Montagna's?" Mr. Topes abruptly asked. "The one with the Donor kneeling in the left-hand corner as if about to kiss the foot of the Child." His spectacles flashed in Mr. Buzzacott's direction.

"Why do you ask?"

"I don't know. I was just thinking of it."

"I think you must mean the one in the Mond Collection."

"Ah yes; very probably. In the Mond . . ."

Barbara opened the door and walked into the twilight of her shuttered room. It was hot even here; for another three hours it would hardly be possible to stir. And that old idiot, Mrs. Topes, always made a fuss if one came in to lunch with bare legs and one's after-bathing tunic. "In India we always made a point of being properly and adequately dressed. An Englishwoman must keep up her position with natives, and to all intents and purposes Italians *are* natives." And so she always had to put on shoes and stockings and a regular frock just at the hottest hour of the day. What an old ass that woman was! She slipped off her clothes as fast as she could. That was a little better.

Standing in front of the long mirror in the wardrobe door she came to the humiliating conclusion that she looked like a piece of badly toasted bread. Brown face, brown neck and shoulders, brown arms, brown legs from the knee downwards; but all the rest of her was white, silly, effeminate, townish white. If only one could run about with no clothes on till one was like those little coppery children who rolled and tumbled in the burning sand! Now she was just underdone, half-baked, and wholly ridiculous. For a long time she looked at her pale image. She saw herself running, bronzed all over, along the sand; or through a field of flowers, narcissus and wild tulips; or in soft grass under grey olive trees. She turned round with a sudden start. There, in the shadows behind her. . . . No, of course there was nothing. It was that awful picture in a magazine she had looked at, so many years ago, when she was a child. There was a lady sitting at her dressing-table, doing her hair in front of the glass; and a huge, hairy black monkey creeping up behind her. She always got the creeps when she looked at herself in a mirror. It was very silly. But still. She turned away from the mirror, crossed the room, and, without lowering the mosquito curtains, lay down on her bed. The flies buzzed about her, settled incessantly on her face. She shook her head, flapped at them angrily with her hands. There would be peace if she let down the netting. But she thought of the Appian Way seen mistily through the bridal veil and preferred to suffer the flies. In the end she had to surrender; the brutes were too much for her. But, at any rate, it wasn't the fear of anophylines that made her lower the netting.

Undisturbed now and motionless, she lay stretched stiffly out under the transparent bell of gauze. A specimen under a glass case. The fancy possessed her mind. She saw a huge museum with thousands of glass cases, full of fossils and butterflies and stuffed birds and mediæval spoons and armour and Florentine jewellery and mummies and carved ivory and illuminated manuscripts. But in one of the cases was a human being, shut up there alive.

All of a sudden she became horribly miserable. " Boring, boring, boring," she whispered, formulating the words aloud. Would it never stop being boring ? The tears came into her eyes. How awful everything was ! And perhaps it would go on being as bad as this all her life. Seventeen from seventy was fifty-three. Fifty-three years of it. And if she lived to a hundred there would be more than eighty.

The thought depressed her all the evening. Even her bathe after tea did her no good. Swimming far out, far out, she lay there, floating on the warm water. Sometimes she looked at the sky, sometimes she turned her head towards the shore. Framed in their pinewoods, the villas looked as small and smug as the advertisement of a seaside resort. But behind them, across the level plain, were the mountains. Sharp, bare peaks of limestone, green woodland slopes and grey-green expanses of terraced olive trees—they seemed marvellously close and clear in this evening light. And beautiful, beautiful beyond words. But that, somehow, only made things worse. And Shelley had lived a few miles farther up the coast, there, behind the headland guarding the Gulf of Spezia. Shelley had been drowned in this milk-warm sea. That made it worse too.

The sun was getting very low and red over the sea. She swam slowly in. On the beach Mrs. Topes waited, disapprovingly. She had known somebody, a strong man, who had caught cramp from staying in too long. He sank like a stone. Like a stone. The queer people Mrs. Topes had known! And the funny things they did, the odd things that happened to them!

Dinner that evening was duller than ever. Barbara went early to bed. All night long the same old irritating cicada scraped and scraped among the pine trees, monotonous and regular as clockwork.

Zip zip, zip zip zip. Boring, boring. Was the animal never bored by its own noise? It seemed odd that it shouldn't be. But, when she came to think of it, nobody ever did get bored with their own noise. Mrs. Topes, for example; she never seemed to get bored. Zip zip, zip zip zip. The cicada went on without a pause.

Concetta knocked at the door at half-past seven. The morning was as bright and cloudless as all the mornings were. Barbara jumped up, looked from one window at the mountains, from the other at the sea; all seemed to be well with them. All was well with her too, this morning. Seated at the mirror, she did not so much as think of the big monkey in the far obscure corner of the room. A bathing dress and a bath-gown, sandals, a handkerchief round her head, and she was ready. Sleep had left no recollection of last night's mortal boredom. She ran downstairs.

"Good morning, Mr. Topes."

Mr. Topes was walking in the garden among the vines. He turned round, took off his hat, smiled a greeting.

"Good morning, Miss Barbara." He paused. Then, with an embarrassed wriggle of introduction he went on; a queer little falter came into his voice. "A real Chaucerian morning, Miss Barbara. A May-day morning — only it happens to be September. Nature is fresh and bright, and there is at least one specimen in this dream garden"—he wriggled more uncomfortably than ever, and there was a tremulous glitter in his round spectacle lenses—"of the poet's 'yonge fresshe folkes.'" He bowed in her direction, smiled deprecatingly, and was silent. The remark, it seemed to him, now that he had finished speaking, was somehow not as good as he had thought it would be.

Barbara laughed. "Chaucer! They used to make us read the *Canterbury Tales* at school. But they always bored me. Are you going to bathe?"

"Not before breakfast." Mr. Topes shook his head. "One is getting a little too old for that."

"Is one?" Why did the silly old man always say 'one' when he meant 'I'? She couldn't help laughing at him. "Well, I must hurry, or else I shall be late for breakfast again, and you know how I catch it."

She ran out, through the gate in the garden wall, across the beach, to the striped red-and-white bathing cabin that stood before the house. Fifty yards away she saw the Marchese Prampolini, still dripping from the sea, running up towards his bathing hut. Catching sight of her, he flashed a smile in her direction, gave a military salute. Barbara waved her hand, then thought that the gesture had been a little too familiar—but at this hour of the morning it was difficult not to have bad jolly manners—and added the corrective of a stiff bow. After all, she had only met him yesterday. Soon she was swimming out to sea, and, ugh! what a lot of horrible huge jelly-fish there were.

Mr. Topes had followed her slowly through the gate and across the sand. He watched her running down from the cabin, slender as a boy, with long, bounding strides. He watched her go jumping with great splashes through the deepening water, then throw herself forward and begin to swim. He watched her till she was no more than a small dark dot far out.

Emerging from his cabin, the marquis met him walking slowly along the beach, his head bent down and his lips slightly moving as though he were repeating something, a prayer or a poem, to himself.

"Good morning, signore." The marquis shook him by the hand with a more than English cordiality.

"Good morning," replied Mr. Topes, allowing his hand to be shaken. He resented this interruption of his thoughts.

"She swims very well, Miss Buzzacott."

"Very," assented Mr. Topes, and smiled to himself to think what beautiful, poetical things he might have said, if he had chosen.

"Well, so, so," said the marquis, too colloquial by half. He shook hands again, and the two men went their respective ways.

Barbara was still a hundred yards from the shore when she heard the crescendo and dying boom of the gong floating out from the villa. Damn! she'd be late again. She quickened her stroke and came splashing out through the shallows, flushed and breathless. She'd be ten minutes late, she calculated; it would take her at least that to do her hair and dress. Mrs. Topes would be on the warpath again; though what business that old woman had to lecture her as she did, goodness only knew. She always succeeded in making herself horribly offensive and unpleasant.

The beach was quite deserted as she trotted, panting, across it, empty to right and left as far as she could see. If only she had a horse to go galloping at the water's edge, miles and miles. Right away down to Bocca d'Arno she'd go, swim the river—she saw herself crouching on the horse's back, as he swam, with legs tucked up on the saddle, trying not to get her feet wet—and gallop on again, goodness only knew where.

In front of the cabin she suddenly halted. There in the ruffled sand she had seen a writing. Big letters, faintly legible, sprawled across her path.

O CLARA D'ELLÉBEUSE.

She pieced the dim letters together. They hadn't been there when she started out to bathe. Who? . . . She looked round. The beach was quite empty. And what was the meaning? "O Clara d'Ellébeuse." She took her bath-gown from the cabin, slipped on her sandals, and ran back towards the house as fast as she could. She felt most horribly frightened.

It was a sultry, headachey sort of morning, with a hot scirocco that stirred the bunting on the flagstaffs. By midday the thunder-clouds had covered half the sky. The sun still blazed on the sea, but over the mountains all was black and indigo. The storm broke noisily overhead just as they were drinking their after-luncheon coffee.

"Arthur," said Mrs. Topes, painfully calm, "shut the shutters, please."

She was not frightened, no. But she preferred not to see the lightning. When the room was darkened, she began to talk, suavely and incessantly.

Lying back in her deep arm-chair, Barbara was thinking of Clara d'Ellébeuse. What did it mean and who was Clara d'Ellébeuse? And why had he written it there for her to see? He—for there could be no doubt who had written it. The flash of teeth and eyes, the military salute; she knew she oughtn't to have waved to him. He had written it there while she was swimming out. Written it and then run away. She rather liked that—just an extraordinary word on the sand, like the footprint in *Robinson Crusoe*.

"Personally," Mrs. Topes was saying, "I prefer Harrod's."

The thunder crashed and rattled. It was rather exhilarating, Barbara thought; one felt, at any rate, that something was happening for a change. She remembered the little room half-way up the stairs at Lady Thingumy's house, with the book-shelves and the green curtains and the orange shade on the light; and that awful young man like a white slug who had tried to kiss her there, at the dance last year. But that was different—not at all serious; and the young man had been so horribly ugly. She saw the marquis running up the beach, quick and alert. Copper coloured all over, with black hair. He was certainly very handsome. But as for being in love, well . . . what did that exactly mean? Perhaps when she knew him better. Even now she fancied she detected something. O Clara d'Ellébeuse. What an extraordinary thing it was!

With his long fingers Mr. Buzzacott combed his beard. This winter, he was thinking, he would put another thousand into Italian money when the exchange was favourable. In the spring it always seemed to drop back again. One could clear three hundred pounds on one's capital if the exchange went down to seventy. The income on three hundred was fifteen pounds a year, and fifteen pounds was now fifteen hundred lire. And fifteen hundred lire, when you came to think of it, was really sixty pounds. That was to say that one would make an addition of more than a pound a week to one's income by this simple little speculation. He became aware that Mrs. Topes had asked him a question.

"Yes, yes, perfectly," he said.

Mrs. Topes talked on; she was keeping up her morale. Was she right in believing that the thunder sounded a little less alarmingly loud and near?

Mr. Topes sat, polishing his spectacles with a white silk handkerchief. Vague and myopic between their puckered lids, his eyes seemed lost, homeless, unhappy. He was thinking about beauty. There were certain relations between the eyelids and the temples, between the breast and the shoulder; there were certain successions of sounds. But what about them? Ah, that was the problem—that was the problem. And there was youth, there was innocence. But it was all very obscure, and there were so many phrases, so many remembered pictures and melodies; he seemed to get himself entangled among them. And he was so old and ineffective.

He put on his spectacles again, and definition came into the foggy world beyond his eyes. The shuttered room was very dark. He could distinguish the Renaissance profile of Mr. Buzzacott, bearded and delicately featured. In her deep arm-chair Barbara appeared, faintly white, in an attitude relaxed and brooding. And Mrs. Topes was nothing more than a voice in the darkness. She had got on to the marriage of the Prince of Wales. Who would they find for him?

Clara d'Ellébeuse, Clara d'Ellébeuse. She saw herself so clearly as the *marchesa.* They would have a house in Rome, a palace. She saw herself in the Palazzo Spada—it had such a lovely vaulted passage leading from the courtyard to the gardens at the back. "MARCHESA PRAMPOLINI, PALAZZO SPADA, ROMA"—a great big visiting-card beautifully engraved. And she would go riding every day in the Pincio. "*Mi porta il mio cavallo,*" she would say to the footman, who answered the bell. *Porta?* Would that be quite correct ? Hardly. She'd have to take some proper Italian lessons to talk to the servants. One must never be ridiculous before servants. "*Voglio il mio cavallo.*" Haughtily one would say it sitting at one's writing-table in a riding-habit, without turning round. It would be a green riding-habit, with a black tricorne hat, braided with silver.

"*Prendero la mia collazione al letto.*" Was that right for breakfast in bed ? Because she would have breakfast in bed, always. And when she got up there would be lovely looking-glasses with three panels where one could see oneself side-face. She saw herself leaning forward, powdering her nose, carefully, scientifically. With the monkey creeping up behind ? Ooh ! Horrible ! *Ho paura di questa scimmia, questo scimmione.*

She would come back to lunch after her ride. Perhaps Prampolini would be there ; she had rather left him out of the picture so far. "*Dov' è il Marchese ?*" "*Nella sala di pranza, signora.*" I began without you, I was so hungry. *Pasta asciutta.* Where have you been, my love ? Riding, my dove. She supposed they'd get into the habit of saying that sort of thing. Everyone seemed to. And you? I have been out with the Fascisti.

Oh, these Fascisti! Would life be worth living when he was always going out with pistols and bombs and things? They would bring him back one day on a stretcher. She saw it. Pale, pale, with blood on him. *Il signore è ferito. Nel petto. Gravamente. E morto.*

How could she bear it? It was too awful; too, too terrible. Her breath came in a kind of sob; she shuddered as though she had been hurt. *E morto. E morto.* The tears came into her eyes.

She was roused suddenly by a dazzling light. The storm had receded far enough into the distance to permit of Mrs. Topes's opening the shutters.

"It's quite stopped raining."

To be disturbed in one's intimate sorrow and self-abandonment at a death-bed by a stranger's intrusion, an alien voice. . . . Barbara turned her face away from the light and surreptitiously wiped her eyes. They might see and ask her why she had been crying. She hated Mrs. Topes for opening the shutters; at the inrush of the light something beautiful had flown, an emotion had vanished, irrecoverably. It was a sacrilege.

Mr. Buzzacott looked at his watch. "Too late, I fear, for a siesta now," he said. "Suppose we ring for an early tea."

"An endless succession of meals," said Mr. Topes, with a tremolo and a sigh. "That's what life seems to be—real life."

"I have been calculating"—Mr. Buzzacott turned his pale green eyes towards his guest—"that I may be able to afford that pretty little *cinque* cassone, after all. It would be a bit of a squeeze." He played with his beard. "But still . . ."

After tea, Barbara and Mr. Topes went for a walk along the beach. She didn't much want to go, but Mrs. Topes thought it would be good for her; so she had to. The storm had passed and the sky over the sea was clear. But the waves were still breaking with an incessant clamour on the outer shallows, driving wide sheets of water high up the beach, twenty or thirty yards above the line where, on a day of calm, the ripples ordinarily expired. Smooth, shining expanses of water advanced and receded like steel surfaces moved out and back by a huge machine.

Through the rain-washed air the mountains appeared with an incredible clarity. Above them hung huge masses of cloud.

"Clouds over Carrara," said Mr. Topes, deprecating his remark with a little shake of the head and a movement of the shoulders. "I like to fancy sometimes that the spirits of the great sculptors lodge among these marble hills, and that it is their unseen hands that carve the clouds into these enormous splendid shapes. I imagine their ghosts"—his voice trembled—"feeling about among superhuman conceptions, planning huge groups and friezes and monumental figures with blowing draperies; planning, conceiving, but never quite achieving. Look, there's something of Michelangelo in that white cloud with the dark shadows underneath it." Mr. Topes pointed, and Barbara nodded and said, "Yes, yes," though she wasn't quite sure which cloud he meant. "It's like Night on the Medici tomb; all the power and the passion are brooding inside it, pent up. And there, in that sweeping, gesticulating piece of vapour—you see the one I mean—there's a Bernini. All the passion's on the surface, expressed; the gesture's caught at its most violent. And that sleek, smug white fellow over there, that's a delicious absurd Canova." Mr. Topes chuckled.

"Why do you always talk about art ?" said Barbara. "You bring these dead people into everything. What do I know about Canova or whoever it is ?" They were none of them alive. She thought of that dark face, bright as a lamp with life. He at least wasn't dead. She wondered whether the letters were still there in the sand before the cabin. No, of course not; the rain and the wind would have blotted them out.

Mr. Topes was silent; he walked with slightly bent knees and his eyes were fixed on the ground; he wore a speckled black-and-white straw hat. He always thought of art; that was what was wrong with him. Like an old tree he was; built up of dead wood, with only a few fibres of life to keep him from rotting away. They walked on for a long time in silence.

"Here's the river," said Mr. Topes at last.

A few steps more and they were on the bank of a wide stream that came down slowly through the plain to the sea. Just inland from the beach it was fringed with pine trees; beyond the trees one could see the plain, and beyond the plain were the mountains. In this calm light after the storm everything looked strange. The colours seemed deeper and more intense than at ordinary times. And though all was so clear, there was a mysterious air of remoteness about the whole scene. There was no sound, except the continuous breathing of the sea. They stood for a little while, looking; then turned back.

Far away along the beach two figures were slowly approaching. White flannel trousers, a pink skirt.

"Nature," Mr. Topes enunciated, with a shake of the head. "One always comes back to nature. At a moment such as this, in surroundings like these, one realises it. One lives now—more quietly, perhaps, but more profoundly. Deep waters. Deep waters. . . ."

The figures drew closer. Wasn't it the marquis? And who was with him? Barbara strained her eyes to see.

"Most of one's life," Mr. Topes went on, "is one prolonged effort to prevent oneself thinking. Your father and I, we collect pictures and read about the dead.

Other people achieve the same result by drinking, or breeding rabbits, or doing amateur carpentry. Anything rather than think calmly about the important things."

Mr. Topes was silent. He looked about him, at the sea, at the mountains, at the great clouds, at his companion. A frail Montagna madonna, with the sea and the westering sun, the mountains and the storm, all eternity as a background. And he was sixty, with all a life, immensely long and yet timelessly short, behind him, an empty life. He thought of death and the miracles of beauty ; behind his round, glittering spectacles he felt inclined to weep.

The approaching couple were quite near now.

"What a funny old walrus," said the lady.

"Walrus ? Your natural history is quite wrong." The marquis laughed. "He's much too dry to be a walrus. I should suggest some sort of an old cat."

"Well, whatever he is, I'm sorry for that poor little girl. Think of having nobody better to go about with ! "

"Pretty, isn't she ? "

"Yes, but too young, of course."

"I like the innocence."

"Innocence? Cher ami! These English girls. Oh, la la! They may look innocent. But, believe me . . ."

"Sh, sh. They'll hear you."

"Pooh, they don't understand Italian."

The marquis raised his hand. "The old walrus . . ." he whispered; then addressed himself loudly and jovially to the newcomers.

"Good evening, signorina. Good evening, Mr. Topes. After a storm the air is always the purest, don't you find, eh?"

Barbara nodded, leaving Mr. Topes to answer. It wasn't his sister. It was the Russian woman, the one of whom Mrs. Topes used to say that it was a disgrace she should be allowed to stay at the hotel. She had turned away, dissociating herself from the conversation; Barbara looked at the line of her averted face. Mr. Topes was saying something about the Pastoral Symphony. Purple face powder in the daylight; it looked hideous.

"Well, au revoir."

The flash of the marquis's smile was directed at them. The Russian woman turned back from the sea, slightly bowed, smiled languidly. Her heavy white eyelids were almost closed; she seemed the prey of an enormous ennui.

"They jar a little," said Mr. Topes when they were out of earshot—"they jar on the time, on the place, on the emotion. They haven't the innocence for this . . . this . . ."—he wriggled and tremoloed out the just, the all too precious word—"this prelapsarian landscape."

He looked sideways at Barbara and wondered what she was so thoughtfully frowning over. Oh, lovely and delicate young creature! What could he adequately say of death and beauty and tenderness? Tenderness . . .

"All this," he went on desperately, and waved his hand to indicate the sky, the sea, the mountains, "this scene is like something remembered, clear and utterly calm; remembered across great gulfs of intervening time."

But that was not really what he wanted to say.

"You see what I mean?" he asked dubiously. She made no reply. How could she see? "This scene is so clear and pure and remote; you need the corresponding emotion. Those people were out of harmony. They weren't clear and pure enough." He seemed to be getting more muddled than ever. "It's an emotion of the young and of the old. You could feel it, I could feel it. Those people couldn't." He was feeling his way through obscurities. Where would he finally arrive? "Certain poems express it. You know Francis Jammes? I have thought so much of his work lately. Art instead of life, as usual; but then I'm made that way. I can't help thinking of Jammes. Those delicate, exquisite things he wrote about Clara d'Ellébeuse."

"Clara d'Ellébeuse?" She stopped and stared at him.

"You know the lines?" Mr. Topes smiled delightedly. "This place makes me think, you make me think of them. '*J'aime dans les temps Clara d'Ellébeuse* . . .' But, my dear Barbara, what is the matter?"

She had started crying, for no reason whatever.

NUNS AT LUNCHEON

NUNS AT LUNCHEON

"WHAT have I been doing since you saw me last?" Miss Penny repeated my question in her loud, emphatic voice. "Well, when did you see me last?"

"It must have been June," I computed.

"Was that after I'd been proposed to by the Russian General?"

"Yes; I remember hearing about the Russian General."

Miss Penny threw back her head and laughed. Her long ear-rings swung and rattled—corpses hanging in chains: an agreeably literary simile. And her laughter was like brass, but that had been said before.

"That was an uproarious incident. It's sad you should have heard of it. I love my Russian General story. '*Vos yeux me rendent fou.*'" She laughed again.

Vos yeux—she had eyes like a hare's, flush with her head and very bright with a superficial and expressionless brightness.

What a formidable woman. I felt sorry for the Russian General.

" '*Sans cœur et sans entrailles*,' " she went on, quoting the poor devil's words. "Such a delightful motto, don't you think? Like '*Sans peur et sans reproche*.' But let me think; what have I been doing since then?" Thoughtfully she bit into the crust of her bread with long, sharp, white teeth.

"Two mixed grills," I said parenthetically to the waiter.

"But of course," exclaimed Miss Penny suddenly. "I haven't seen you since my German trip. All sorts of adventures. My appendicitis; my nun."

"Your nun?"

"My marvellous nun. I must tell you all about her."

"Do." Miss Penny's anecdotes were always curious. I looked forward to an entertaining luncheon.

"You knew I'd been in Germany this autumn?"

"Well, I didn't, as a matter of fact. But still——"

"I was just wandering round." Miss Penny described a circle in the air with her gaudily jewelled hand. She always twinkled with massive and improbable jewellery. " Wandering round, living on three pounds a week, partly amusing myself, partly collecting materials for a few little articles. 'What it Feels Like to be a Conquered Nation'—sob-stuff for the Liberal press, you know—and 'How the Hun is Trying to Wriggle out of the Indemnity,' for the other fellows. One has to make the best of all possible worlds, don't you find ? But we mustn't talk shop. Well, I was wandering round, and very pleasant I found it. Berlin, Dresden, Leipzig. Then down to Munich and all over the place. One fine day I got to Grauburg. You know Grauburg ? It's one of those picture-book German towns with a castle on a hill, hanging beer-gardens, a Gothic church, an old university, a river, a pretty bridge, and forests all round. Charming. But I hadn't much opportunity to appreciate the beauties of the place. The day after I arrived there—bang !—I went down with appendicitis—screaming, I may add."

" But how appalling ! "

" They whisked me off to hospital, and cut me open before you could say knife. Excellent surgeon, highly efficient Sisters of Charity to nurse me—I couldn't have been in better hands. But it was a bore being tied there by the leg for four weeks—a great bore. Still, the thing had its compensations. There was my nun, for example. Ah, here's the food, thank Heaven!"

The mixed grill proved to be excellent. Miss Penny's description of the nun came to me in scraps and snatches. A round, pink, pretty face in a winged coif; blue eyes and regular features; teeth altogether too perfect—false, in fact; but the general effect extremely pleasing. A youthful Teutonic twenty-eight.

"She wasn't my nurse," Miss Penny explained. "But I used to see her quite often when she came in to have a look at the *tolle Engländerin*. Her name was Sister Agatha. During the war, they told me, she had converted any number of wounded soldiers to the true faith—which wasn't surprising, considering how pretty she was."

"Did she try and convert you?" I asked.

"She wasn't such a fool." Miss Penny laughed, and rattled the miniature gallows of her ears.

I amused myself for a moment with the

thought of Miss Penny's conversion—Miss Penny confronting a vast assembly of Fathers of the Church, rattling her earrings at their discourses on the Trinity, laughing her appalling laugh at the doctrine of the Immaculate Conception, meeting the stern look of the Grand Inquisitor with a flash of her bright, emotionless hare's eyes. What was the secret of the woman's formidableness ?

But I was missing the story. What had happened ? Ah yes, the gist of it was that Sister Agatha had appeared one morning, after two or three days' absence, dressed, not as a nun, but in the overalls of a hospital charwoman, with a handkerchief instead of a winged coif on her shaven head.

" Dead," said Miss Penny ; " she looked as though she were dead. A walking corpse, that's what she was. It was a shocking sight. I shouldn't have thought it possible for anyone to change so much in so short a time. She walked painfully, as though she had been ill for months, and she had great burnt rings round her eyes and deep lines in her face. And the general expression of unhappiness—that was something quite appalling."

She leaned out into the gangway between the two rows of tables, and caught the passing waiter by the end of one of his coat-tails. The little Italian looked round with an expression of surprise that deepened into terror on his face.

"Half a pint of Guinness," ordered Miss Penny. "And, after this, bring me some jam roll."

"No jam roll to-day, madam."

"Damn!" said Miss Penny. "Bring me what you like, then."

She let go of the waiter's tail, and resumed her narrative.

"Where was I? Yes, I remember. She came into my room, I was telling you, with a bucket of water and a brush, dressed like a charwoman. Naturally I was rather surprised. 'What on earth are you doing, Sister Agatha?' I asked. No answer. She just shook her head, and began to scrub the floor. When she'd finished, she left the room without so much as looking at me again. 'What's happened to Sister Agatha?' I asked my nurse when she next came in. 'Can't say.'—'Won't say,' I said. No answer. It took me nearly a week to find out what really had happened. Nobody dared tell me ; it was *strengst verboten*, as they used to say in the good old days. But I wormed it out in the long run. My nurse, the doctor, the charwomen—I got something out of all of them. I always get what I want in the end." Miss Penny laughed like a horse.

"I'm sure you do," I said politely.

"Much obliged," acknowledged Miss Penny. "But to proceed. My information came to me in fragmentary whispers. 'Sister Agatha ran away with a man.' —Dear me!—'One of the patients.'—You don't say so.—'A criminal out of the jail.'—The plot thickens.—'He ran away from her.'—It seems to grow thinner again.—'They brought her back here ; she's been disgraced. There's been a funeral service for her in the chapel—coffin and all. She had to be present at it—her own funeral. She isn't a nun any more. She has to do charwoman's work now, the roughest in the hospital. She's not allowed to speak to anybody, and nobody's allowed to speak to her. She's regarded as dead.'" Miss Penny paused to signal to the harassed little Italian. "My small 'Guinness,'" she called out.

"Coming, coming," and the foreign voice cried "Guinness" down the lift, and from below another voice echoed, "Guinness."

"I filled in the details bit by bit. There was our hero, to begin with; I had to bring him into the picture, which was rather difficult, as I had never seen him. But I got a photograph of him. The police circulated one when he got away; I don't suppose they ever caught him." Miss Penny opened her bag. "Here it is," she said. "I always carry it about with me; it's become a superstition. For years, I remember, I used to carry a little bit of heather tied up with string. Beautiful, isn't it? There's a sort of Renaissance look about it, don't you think? He was half-Italian, you know."

Italian. Ah, that explained it. I had been wondering how Bavaria could have produced this thin-faced creature with the big dark eyes, the finely modelled nose and chin, and the fleshy lips so royally and sensually curved.

"He's certainly very superb," I said, handing back the picture.

Miss Penny put it carefully away in her

bag. "Isn't he?" she said. "Quite marvellous. But his character and his mind were even better. I see him as one of those innocent, childlike monsters of iniquity who are simply unaware of the existence of right and wrong. And he had genius—the real Italian genius for engineering, for dominating and exploiting nature. A true son of the Roman aqueduct builders he was, and a brother of the electrical engineers. Only Kuno—that was his name—didn't work in water; he worked in women. He knew how to harness the natural energy of passion; he made devotion drive his mills. The commercial exploitation of love-power, that was his speciality. I sometimes wonder," Miss Penny added in a different tone, "whether I shall ever be exploited, when I get a little more middle-aged and celibate, by one of these young engineers of the passions. It would be humiliating, particularly as I've done so little exploiting from my side."

She frowned and was silent for a moment. No, decidedly, Miss Penny was not beautiful; you could not even honestly say that she had charm or was attractive. That high Scotch colouring, those hare's eyes, the voice, the terrifying laugh, and the size of her, the general formidableness of the woman. No, no, no.

" You said he had been in prison," I said. The silence, with all its implications, was becoming embarrassing.

Miss Penny sighed, looked up, and nodded. " He was fool enough," she said, " to leave the straight and certain road of female exploitation for the dangerous courses of burglary. We all have our occasional accesses of folly. They gave him a heavy sentence, but he succeeded in getting pneumonia, I think it was, a week after entering jail. He was transferred to the hospital. Sister Agatha, with her known talent for saving souls, was given him as his particular attendant. But it was he, I'm afraid, who did the converting."

Miss Penny finished off the last mouthful of the ginger pudding which the waiter had brought in lieu of jam roll.

" I suppose you don't smoke cheroots," I said, as I opened my cigar-case.

" Well, as a matter of fact, I do," Miss Penny replied. She looked sharply round the restaurant. " I must just see if there are any of those horrible little gossip paragraphers here to-day. One doesn't want to figure in the social and personal column to-morrow morning: 'A fact which is not so generally known as it ought to be, is that Miss Penny, the well-known woman journalist, always ends her luncheon with a six-inch Burma cheroot. I saw her yesterday in a restaurant—not a hundred miles from Carmelite Street—smoking like a house on fire.' You know the touch. But the coast seems to be clear, thank goodness."

She took a cheroot from the case, lit it at my proffered match, and went on talking.

"Yes, it was young Kuno who did the converting. Sister Agatha was converted back into the worldly Melpomene Fugger she had been before she became the bride of holiness."

"Melpomene Fugger?"

"That was her name. I had her history from my old doctor. He had seen all Grauburg, living and dying and propagating, for generations. Melpomene Fugger—why, he had brought little Melpel into the world, little Melpchen. Her father was Professor Fugger, the great Professor Fugger, the *berûmter*

Geolog. Oh yes, of course, I know the name. So well . . . He was the man who wrote the standard work on Lemuria—you know, the hypothetical continent where the lemurs come from. I showed due respect. Liberal-minded he was, a disciple of Herder, a world-burgher, as they beautifully call it over there. Anglophile, too, and always ate porridge for breakfast—up till August 1914. Then, on the radiant morning of the fifth, he renounced it for ever, solemnly and with tears in his eyes. The national food of a people who had betrayed culture and civilisation—how could he go on eating it? It would stick in his throat. In future he would have a lightly boiled egg. He sounded, I thought, altogether charming. And his daughter, Melpomene—she sounded charming, too; and such thick, yellow pigtails when she was young! Her mother was dead, and a sister of the great Professor's ruled the house with an iron rod. Aunt Bertha was her name. Well, Melpomene grew up, very plump and appetising. When she was seventeen, something very odious and disagreeable happened to her. Even the doctor didn't know exactly what it was; but he wouldn't have been surprised if it had had something to do with the then Professor of Latin, an old friend of the family's, who combined, it seems, great erudition with a horrid fondness for very young ladies."

Miss Penny knocked half an inch of cigar ash into her empty glass.

"If I wrote short stories," she went on reflectively "(but it's too much bother), I should make this anecdote into a sort of potted life history, beginning with a scene immediately after this disagreeable event in Melpomene's life. I see the scene so clearly. Poor little Melpel is leaning over the bastions of Grauburg Castle, weeping into the June night and the mulberry trees in the gardens thirty feet below. She is besieged by the memory of what happened this dreadful afternoon. Professor Engelmann, her father's old friend, with the magnificent red Assyrian beard . . . Too awful—too awful! But then, as I was saying, short stories are really too much bother; or perhaps I'm too stupid to write them. I bequeath it to you. You know how to tick these things off."

"You're generous."

"Not at all," said Miss Penny. "My terms are a ten per cent commission on the American sale. Incidentally there won't be an American sale. Poor Melpchen's history is not for the chaste public of Those States. But let me hear what you propose to do with Melpomene now you've got her on the castle bastions."

"That's simple," I said. "I know all about German university towns and castles on hills. I shall make her look into the June night, as you suggest; into the violet night with its points of golden flame. There will be the black silhouette of the castle, with its sharp roofs and hooded turrets, behind her. From the hanging beer-gardens in the town below the voices of the students, singing in perfect four-part harmony, will float up through the dark-blue spaces. '*Röslein, Röslein, Röslein rot*' and '*Das Ringlein sprang in zwei*'—the heart-rendingly sweet old songs will make her cry all the more. Her tears will patter like rain among the leaves of the mulberry trees in the garden below. Does that seem to you adequate?"

"Very nice," said Miss Penny. "But how are you going to bring the sex problem and all its horrors into your landscape?"

"Well, let me think." I called to memory those distant foreign summers when I was completing my education. "I know. I shall suddenly bring a swarm of moving candles and Chinese lanterns under the mulberry trees. You imagine the rich lights and shadows, the jewel-bright leafage, the faces and moving limbs of men and women, seen for an instant and gone again. They are students and girls of the town come out to dance, this windless, blue June night, under the mulberry trees. And now they begin, thumping round and round in a ring, to the music of their own singing:

> '*Wir können spielen*
> *Vio-vio-vio-lin,*
> *Wir können spielen*
> *Vi-o-lin.*'

Now the rhythm changes, quickens:

> '*Und wir können tanzen Bumstarara,*
> *Bumstarara, Bumstarara,*
> *Und wir können tanzen Bumstarara,*
> *Bumstarara-rara.*'

The dance becomes a rush, an elephantine prancing on the dry lawn under the mulberry trees. And from the bastion

Melpomene looks down and perceives, suddenly and apocalyptically, that everything in the world is sex, sex, sex. Men and women, male and female—always the same, and all, in the light of the horror of the afternoon, disgusting. That's how I should do it, Miss Penny."

"And very nice, too. But I wish you could find a place to bring in my conversation with the doctor. I shall never forget the way he cleared his throat and coughed before embarking on the delicate subject. 'You may know, ahem, gracious Miss,' he began—'you may know that religious phenomena are often, ahem, closely connected with sexual causes.' I replied that I had heard rumours which might justify me in believing this to be true among Roman Catholics, but that in the Church of England—and I for one was a practitioner of Anglicanismus—it was very different. That might be, said the doctor; he had had no opportunity in the course of his long medical career of personally studying Anglicanismus. But he could vouch for the fact that among his patients, here in Grauburg, mysticismus was very often mixed up with the *Geschlechtsleben*. Melpomene was a case in point. After that hateful afternoon she had become extremely religious; the Professor of Latin had diverted her emotions out of their normal channels. She rebelled against the placid Agnosticismus of her father, and at night, in secret, when Aunt Bertha's dragon eyes were closed, she would read such forbidden books as *The Life of St. Theresa*, *The Little Flowers of St. Francis*, *The Imitation of Christ*, and the horribly enthralling *Book of Martyrs*. Aunt Bertha confiscated these works whenever she came upon them; she considered them more pernicious than the novels of Marcel Prévost. The character of a good potential housewife might be completely undermined by reading of this kind. It was rather a relief for Melpomene when Aunt Bertha shuffled off, in the summer of 1911, this mortal coil. She was one of those indispensables of whom one makes the discovery, when they are gone, that one can get on quite as well without them. Poor Aunt Bertha!"

"One can imagine Melpomene trying to believe she was sorry, and horribly ashamed to find that she was really, in secret, almost glad." The suggestion seemed to me ingenious, but Miss Penny accepted it as obvious.

"Precisely," she said; "and the emotion would only further confirm and give new force to the tendencies which her aunt's death left her free to indulge as much as she liked. Remorse, contrition—they would lead to the idea of doing penance. And for one who was now wallowing in the martyrology, penance was the mortification of the flesh. She used to kneel for hours, at night, in the cold; she ate too little, and when her teeth ached, which they often did,—for she had a set, the doctor told me, which had given trouble from the very first,—she would not go and see the dentist, but lay awake at night, savouring to the full her excruciations, and feeling triumphantly that they must, in some strange way, be pleasing to the Mysterious Powers. She went on like that for two or three years, till she was poisoned through and through. In the end she went down with gastric ulcer. It was three months before she came out of hospital, well for the first time in a long space of years, and with a brand new set of imperishable teeth, all gold and ivory. And in mind, too, she was changed—for the better, I suppose. The nuns who nursed her had made her see that in mortifying herself she had acted supererogatively and through spiritual pride; instead of doing right, she had sinned. The only road to salvation, they told her, lay in discipline, in the orderliness of established religion, in obedience to authority. Secretly, so as not to distress her poor father, whose Agnosticismus was extremely dogmatic, for all its unobtrusiveness, Melpomene became a Roman Catholic. She was twenty-two. Only a few months later came the war and Professor Fugger's eternal renunciation of porridge. He did not long survive the making of that patriotic gesture. In the autumn of 1914 he caught a fatal influenza. Melpomene was alone in the world. In the spring of 1915 there was a new and very conscientious Sister of Charity at work among the wounded in the hospital of Grauburg. Here," explained Miss Penny, jabbing the air with her forefinger, "you put a line of asterisks or dots to signify a six years' gulf in the narrative. And you begin again right in the middle of a dialogue between Sister Agatha and the newly convalescent Kuno."

"What's their dialogue to be about?" I asked.

"Oh, that's easy enough," said Miss Penny. "Almost anything would do. What about this, for example? You explain that the fever has just abated; for the first time for days the young man is fully conscious. He feels himself to be well, reborn, as it were, in a new world—a world so bright and novel and jolly that he can't help laughing at the sight of it. He looks about him; the flies on the ceiling strike him as being extremely comic. How do they manage to walk upside down? They have suckers on their feet, says Sister Agatha, and wonders if her natural history is quite sound. Suckers on their feet—ha, ha! What an uproarious notion! Suckers on their feet—that's good, that's damned good! You can say charming, pathetic, positively tender things about the irrelevant mirth of convalescents—the more so in this particular case, where the mirth is expressed by a young man who is to be taken back to jail as soon as he can stand firmly on his legs. Ha, ha! Laugh on, unhappy boy! It is the quacking of the Fates, the Parcæ, the Norns!"

Miss Penny gave an exaggerated imitation of her own brassy laughter. At the sound of it the few lunchers who still lingered at the other tables looked up, startled.

"You can write pages about Destiny and its ironic quacking. It's tremendously impressive, and there's money in every line."

"You may be sure I shall."

"Good! Then I can get on with my story. The days pass and the first hilarity of convalescence fades away. The young man remembers and grows sullen; his strength comes back to him, and with it a sense of despair. His mind broods incessantly on the hateful future. As for the consolations of religion, he won't listen to them. Sister Agatha perseveres—oh, with what anxious solicitude!—in the attempt to make him understand and believe and be comforted. It is all so tremendously important, and in this case, somehow, more important than in any other. And now you see the *Geschlechtsleben* working yeastily and obscurely, and once again the quacking of the Norns is audible. By the way," said Miss Penny, changing her tone and leaning confidentially across the table, "I wish you'd tell me something. Do you really—honestly, I mean—do you seriously believe in literature?"

"Believe in literature?"

"I was thinking," Miss Penny explained, "of Ironic Fate and the quacking of the Norns and all that."

"'M yes."

"And then there's this psychology and introspection business; and construction and good narrative and word pictures and *le mot juste* and verbal magic and striking metaphors."

I remembered that I had compared Miss Penny's tinkling ear-rings to skeletons hanging in chains.

"And then, finally, and to begin with —Alpha and Omega—there's ourselves: two professionals gloating, with an absolute lack of sympathy, over a seduced nun, and speculating on the best method of turning her misfortunes into cash. It's all very curious, isn't it?—when one begins to think about it dispassionately."

"Very curious," I agreed. "But, then, so is everything else if you look at it like that."

"No, no," said Miss Penny. "Nothing's so curious as our business. But I shall never get to the end of my story if I get started on first principles."

Miss Penny continued her narrative. I was still thinking of literature. Do you believe in it? Seriously? Ah! Luckily the question was quite meaningless. The story came to me rather vaguely, but it seemed that the young man was getting better; in a few more days, the doctor had said, he would be well—well enough to go back to jail. No, no. The question was meaningless. I would think about it no more. I concentrated my attention again.

"Sister Agatha," I heard Miss Penny saying, "prayed, exhorted, indoctrinated. Whenever she had half a minute to spare from her other duties she would come running into the young man's room. 'I wonder if you fully realise the importance of prayer?' she would ask, and, before he had time to answer, she would give him a breathless account of the uses and virtues of regular and patient supplication. Or else it was: 'May I tell you about St. Theresa?' or 'St. Stephen, the first martyr—you know about him, don't you?' Kuno simply wouldn't listen at first. It seemed so fantastically irrelevant, such an absurd interruption to his thoughts, his serious, despairing thoughts about the future. Prison was real, imminent, and this woman buzzed about him with her ridiculous fairy-tales. Then, suddenly, one day he began to listen, he showed signs of contrition and conversion. Sister Agatha announced her triumph to the other nuns, and there was rejoicing over the one lost sheep. Melpomene had never felt so happy in her life, and Kuno, looking at her radiant face, must have wondered how he could have been such a fool as not to see from the first what was now so obvious. The woman had lost her head about him. And he had only four days now—four days in which to tap the tumultuous love power, to canalise it, to set it working for his escape. Why hadn't he started a week ago? He could have made certain of it then. But now? There was no knowing. Four days was a horribly short time."

"How did he do it?" I asked, for Miss Penny had paused.

"That's for you to say," she replied, and shook her ear-rings at me. "I don't know. Nobody knows, I imagine, except the two parties concerned and perhaps Sister Agatha's confessor. But one can reconstruct the crime, as they say. How would you have done it? You're a man, you ought to be familiar with the processes of amorous engineering."

"You flatter me," I answered. "Do you seriously suppose——" I extended my arms. Miss Penny laughed like a horse. "No. But, seriously, it's a problem. The case is a very special one. The person, a nun; the place, a hospital; the opportunities, few. There could be no favourable circumstances—no moonlight, no distant music; and any form of direct attack would be sure to fail. That audacious confidence which is your amorist's best weapon would be useless here."

"Obviously," said Miss Penny. "But there are surely other methods. There is the approach through pity and the maternal instincts. And there's the approach through Higher Things, through the soul. Kuno must have worked on those lines, don't you think? One can imagine him letting himself be converted, praying with her, and at the same time appealing for her sympathy and even threatening—with a great air of seriousness—to kill himself rather than go back to jail. You can write that up easily and convincingly enough. But it's the sort of thing that bores me so frightfully to do. That's why I can never bring myself to write fiction. What is the point of it all? And the way you literary men think yourselves so important—particularly if you write tragedies. It's all very queer, very queer indeed."

I made no comment. Miss Penny changed her tone and went on with the narrative.

"Well," she said, "whatever the means employed, the engineering process was perfectly successful. Love was made to find out a way. On the afternoon before Kuno was to go back to prison, two Sisters of Charity walked out of the hospital gates, crossed the square in front of it, glided down the narrow streets towards the river, boarded a tram at the bridge, and did not descend till the car had reached its terminus in the farther suburbs. They began to walk briskly along the high road out into the country. 'Look!' said one of them, when they were clear of the houses; and with the gesture of a conjurer produced from nowhere a red leather purse. 'Where did it come from?' asked the other, opening her eyes. Memories of Elisha and the ravens, of the widow's cruse, of the loaves and fishes, must have floated through the radiant fog in poor Melpomene's mind. 'The old lady I was sitting next to in the tram left her bag open. Nothing could have been simpler.' 'Kuno! You don't mean to say you stole it?' Kuno swore horribly. He had opened the purse. 'Only sixty marks. Who'd have thought that an old camel, all dressed up in silk and furs, would only have sixty marks in her purse. And I must have a thousand at least to get away.' It's easy to reconstruct the rest of the conversation down to the inevitable, 'For God's sake, shut up,' with which Kuno put an end to Melpomene's dismayed moralising. They trudge on in silence. Kuno thinks desperately. Only sixty marks; he can do nothing with that. If only he had something to sell, a piece of jewellery, some gold or silver—anything, anything. He knows such a good place for selling things. Is he to be caught again for lack of a few marks? Melpomene is also thinking. Evil must often be done that good may follow. After all, had not she herself stolen Sister Mary of the Purification's clothes when she was asleep after night duty ? Had not she run away from the convent, broken her vows ? And yet how convinced she was that she was doing rightly ! The mysterious Powers emphatically approved ; she felt sure of it. And now there was the red purse. But what was a red purse in comparison with a saved soul—and, after all, what was she doing but saving Kuno's soul ? " Miss Penny, who had adopted the voice and gestures of a debater asking rhetorical questions, brought her hand with a slap on to the table. " Lord, what a bore this sort of stuff is ! " she exclaimed. " Let's get to the end of this dingy anecdote as quickly as possible. By this time, you must imagine, the shades of night were falling fast—the chill November twilight, and so on ; but I leave the natural descriptions to you. Kuno gets into the ditch at the roadside and takes off his robes. One imagines that he would feel himself safer in trousers, more capable of acting with decision in a crisis. They tramp on for miles. Late in the evening they leave the high road and strike up through the fields towards the forest. At the fringe of the wood they find one of those wheeled huts where the shepherds sleep in the lambing season.

"The real 'Maison du Berger.'"

"Precisely," said Miss Penny, and she began to recite:

> 'Si ton coeur gémissant du poids de notre vie
> Se traine et se débat comme un aigle blessé. . . .'

How does it go on? I used to adore it all so much when I was a girl:

> 'Le seuil est perfumé, l'alcôve est large et sombre,
> Et là parmi les fleurs, nous trouverons dans l'ombre
> Pour nos cheveux unis un lit silencieux.'

I could go on like this indefinitely."

"Do," I said.

"No, no. No, no. I'm determined to finish this wretched story. Kuno broke the padlock of the door. They entered. What happened in that little hut?" Miss Penny leaned forward at me. Her large hare's eyes glittered, the long ear-rings swung and faintly tinkled. "Imagine the emotions of a virgin of thirty, and a nun at that, in the terrifying presence of desire. Imagine the easy, familiar brutalities of the young man. Oh, there's pages to be made out of this—the absolutely impenetrable darkness, the smell of straw, the voices, the strangled crying, the movements! And one likes to fancy that the emotions pulsing about in that confined space made palpable vibrations like a deep sound that shakes the air. Why, it's ready-made literature, this scene. In the morning," Miss Penny went on, after a pause, "two woodcutters on their way to work noticed that the door of the hut was ajar. They approached the hut cautiously, their axes raised and ready for a blow if there should be need of it. Peeping in, they saw a woman in a black dress lying face downwards in the straw. Dead? No; she moved, she moaned. 'What's the matter?' A blubbered face, smeared with streaks of tear-clotted grey dust, is lifted towards them. 'What's the matter?'—'He's gone!' What a queer, indistinct utterance. The woodcutters regard one another. What does she say? She's a foreigner, perhaps. 'What's the matter?' they repeat once more. The woman bursts out violently crying. 'Gone, gone! He's gone,' she sobs out in her vague, inarticulate way. 'Oh, gone. That's what she says. Who's gone ? '—' He's left me.'—' What ? '—' Left me . . .'—' What the devil . . . ? Speak a little more distinctly.'—' I can't,' she wails ; ' he's taken my teeth.'—' Your what ? '—' My teeth ! '—and the shrill voice breaks into a scream, and she falls back sobbing into the straw. The woodcutters look significantly at one another. They nod. One of them applies a thick yellow-nailed forefinger to his forehead."

Miss Penny looked at her watch.

" Good heavens ! " she said, " it's nearly half-past three. I must fly. Don't forget about the funeral service," she added, as she put on her coat. " The tapers, the black coffin in the middle of the aisle, the nuns in their white-winged coifs, the gloomy chanting, and the poor cowering creature without any teeth, her face all caved in like an old woman's, wondering whether she wasn't really and in fact dead—wondering whether she wasn't already in hell. Good-bye."

Printed in Great Britain
at Hopetoun Street, Edinburgh,
by T. and A. CONSTABLE LTD.
Printers to the University of Edinburgh